Mr Meachin

Given to me by
a teacher who was given
these books by a girl over
her road and he put it
in the school library.
At the end of the
year when we broke
up and Mr Meachin
retired, I was given
this book.

Heather Pindar

# Ponies at Westways

# *Ponies at Westways*

## CONSTANCE M. WHITE

HUTCHINSON OF LONDON

HUTCHINSON & CO. (*Publishers*) LTD
*178–202 Great Portland Street, London, W.1*

London Melbourne Sydney
Auckland Bombay Toronto
Johannesburg New York

★

*Third Impression 1959*

TO

# ANNE

Who asked for horses

*This book has been set in Baskerville type
face. It has been printed in Great Britain by
Taylor Garnett Evans & Co. Ltd., Watford,
Herts, and bound by them*

# CONTENTS

## Unwelcome News

THE summer term at Westways school was already two weeks old. Terry Barton, a merry-looking girl with dark-brown hair cut in a straight fringe above her wide grey eyes, came running swiftly down the stairs into the square hall. She had defeated the usual Monday morning scramble with unexpected success and now she sped across the garden, past the orchard and through a white gate leading to the stables.

The loose boxes were built around a cobbled yard, and here several girls in blue overalls were working busily. One or two hailed Terry as she passed, but she only nodded smilingly and made her way to the box in the far corner where a chestnut pony was being tended by a red-haired girl with a freckled face.

'How is Cobber this morning, Sheila?' Terry asked her anxiously.

'Oh, he's much better, Terry! Masters says that slight lameness has quite gone and he's all right to ride, only we must deal gently with him for a bit.'

'That's fine. Good old boy, aren't you, Cobber?' Terry fondled the soft brown nose that the pony pushed into her hand. From the next box came an impatient stamping and Terry put her head over the door and said laughingly :

'All right, Dallas. I know I should have said good morning to you as well.' She patted the pony's dark-brown coat and told Sheila seriously, 'Rosemary and I could never make up our minds which we liked best.'

'Have you heard from Rosemary yet?'

Terry frowned.

'No. That reminds me, the postman must have been by now and there might be a letter. I must go.'

As she ran back across the garden, Terry reflected that it was really strange that she hadn't heard from Rosemary again. What could be happening?

There were several girls in the hall and Terry stood beside them, scanning the names on the letters in the rack. Someone behind her reached out a long arm and extracted a letter with a little whoop of triumph, then tossed an envelope across.

'Sorry, Terry, this is yours. I pulled it out with mine.'

'Thanks, Pat.' Terry pounced on the letter eagerly and slit it open. It was Rosemary's writing. Now she would know what was the matter and why her friend's arrival back at school had been so long delayed. In her previous letter Rosemary had been so maddeningly mysterious.

Beyond the wide-open door leading to the porch the morning sunlight streamed across the garden and painted the mounting North Devon moors beyond with golden colours. Terry walked slowly towards the door, her eyes on the closely written pages of Rosemary's letter. As she read, her expression became more and more dismayed. Presently she folded the letter and, hurrying out into the garden again, took a quiet path leading towards the shrubbery, avoiding someone behind her who called her name. The enthusiasm with which she had begun the day was completely gone. She could think only of the unpleasant news she had just received.

Presently the first blank feeling of misery eased a little. With a sudden desire for the sympathy of those who would understand, Terry turned and, going into the house, ran upstairs to the dormitory which she now shared with only two of her friends. Though it was but a short while since she had left her companions to finish their dressing, it was as though her bad news had created a gulf of time. Terry opened the door, and her glance fell on the empty cubicle in the corner with a sick feeling of dismay. She steadied her voice so that it was carefully devoid of expression.

'I say, girls, I've just had a letter from Rosemary. She's not coming back.'

The other two girls stared at her incredulously.

'Not coming back? Do you mean . . . not at all?' Jennifer Lee, fair-haired and blue-eyed, was commonly called 'Tiny' in friendly derision of her unusual height. She repeated Terry's words blankly now in the small sweet voice which was such a surprising contradiction of her size, and sank limply on to the bed as if the effort to understand such a disaster exhausted her. Elizabeth Friend, a plump, jolly-looking girl with glasses who wore her dark curly hair at shoulder length, protested anxiously:

'Terry, you can't really mean that! Do let us see the letter. *Why* isn't she coming back?'

Terry threw the letter across with a careless flourish and sank into a chair dejectedly.

'Mr. Lowman has been offered a job in Ireland and they've decided to take Rosemary with them and send her to school there. You remember she said in her last letter that the family plans had changed suddenly and she wasn't allowed to tell us about it until everything was settled. But I never imagined anything like this! Isn't it sickening? We've missed her so dreadfully these last two weeks!' Terry bent her head and retied a shoelace vigorously to hide the momentary trembling of her lips.

For a few minutes there was absolute silence while each one of the trio reflected blankly what Rosemary's permanent absence would mean.

'Well, that's split up the Friendleebarlows for good, hasn't it?' muttered Jennifer in a gloomy voice. 'And you remember, Terry, when we put our sur-names together two years ago we vowed the Friendleebarlows would be pals right through the school.'

'I thought we'd even be each other's bridesmaids!' wailed Elizabeth so tragically that even Terry forgot her woes for a moment and the corners of her mouth twitched upwards and her grey eyes twinkled wickedly.

'Just listen to poor Dumpling! Can't you imagine her a bridesmaid, or a bride?' She chanted derisively under her breath to the tune of 'Wedding March':

'Here comes the bride,
All fat and wide.
Can't see the bridegroom
For size of the bride.'

'Oh, you are mean, Terry! Mummy says this is only puppy fat and I shall probably be quite a sylph in a few years' time!' protested her victim indignantly. Over Terry's head she and Jennifer exchanged a glance of understanding. It was something of a relief to find that Terry could still joke, for though they would miss Rosemary pretty badly themselves, it was even worse, they knew, for Terry. Those two had been inseparable from kindergarten days.

At this moment the breakfast-bell cut short further lamentations, for Miss Duncan, the Headmistress, though indulgent enough in some ways, was very strict regarding punctuality at meals.

In the long panelled dining-hall downstairs the three girls took their places at the Fourth Form table, where the news was received with universal dismay, for Rosemary had been popular with everyone.

'All the same, I can somehow imagine Rosemary in Ireland,' remarked Pat Hemmings thoughtfully. 'The harum-scarum type, don't you know.'

'She always found plenty of scope here,' commented Terry tersely, rapidly spooning porridge.

'Well, travel broadens the mind, anyway. I feel mine needs broadening!' Pat heaved a tremendous sigh and everyone laughed. 'Seriously, though, I rather envy her. I've never been to Ireland, and I believe it's very beautiful. Actually I haven't been anywhere but home and here, unless you count the summer holidays, and then we nearly always go to my aunt's farm in Cornwall.'

Beryl Stanley, a new girl that term, shook back her curly black hair with a self-conscious gesture.

'When I leave here I'm going to travel in Europe for a year. Mummy and Daddy say they think everyone should as part of their education.'

'Maybe they should, but everyone hasn't the money for such luxuries,' Terry said forbiddingly. None of the Fourth were very keen on Beryl, who had obviously been spoiled and thought far too much of herself altogether. In any case, Terry felt she didn't want to talk about Rosemary any more, and changing the subject deliberately she told the others: 'Shelia says Cobber is much better and Masters says we can ride him. It was the Third's morning for grooming, but I just had time to run down to the stables before breakfast.'

'Wonder of wonders! Couldn't you sleep?' taunted Pat.

'I can't think why Miss Duncan makes us groom the horses ourselves,' complained Beryl, with an injured air. 'It's such a horrible job.'

There was a chorus of disagreement, and Terry said bluntly:

'You can't be really fond of horses. Most of us love it. Besides, Masters is so short-handed that he is glad of our help. I look forward to our turn, except that sometimes it's hard to get up a whole hour earlier than usual. I never mind once I *am* up.'

Beryl was determined to grumble.

'Well, I know I'm going to keep out of Dallas' way in future. He almost kicked me the other morning. He's vicious.'

'Oh, Beryl, he isn't!' Several voices defended the pony's reputation, and Jennifer added shrewdly, 'Dallas has a lot of spirit, and the way some of the kids pull at his mouth I don't wonder he kicks.'

'If that remark was intended for me, Tiny, I'd like to inform you that when Dallas tried to kick *me* I'd just given him a decent feed,' Beryl asserted aggrievedly.

'Bet you were trying to groom him at the same time, then, so that it wouldn't take you so long.' Terry laughed. 'How would you like someone to wash your face and comb your hair all the time you were having breakfast? But there,' she added pityingly, 'I guess you didn't have much to do with horses before you came to Westways.'

'Not with grooming them, although of course I had good riding-lessons at the school. Anyway'—Beryl tossed her head importantly—'I'm going to ask Daddy to let me have a pony of my own. I don't see how I can get on with my riding when I have to use these moorland ponies that everyone else hacks about. And I shall ask Dad to see that I get a decent blood pony.'

'Well——!' Terry's indignant remarks were, perhaps fortunately, cut short by Miss Duncan, who at that moment gave the signal for grace. With a scraping of feet and clattering of chairs the pupils of Westways trooped out of the dining-room.

Up in Dormitory Ten the three friends busied themselves with making their beds and tidying the room, inevitably returning to the sad fact of Rosemary's desertion.

'Well, there's just one good thing about it.' Jennifer shook up a pillow vigorously, her expression brightening. 'We're not likely to have anyone else in here with us now, thank goodness.' She glanced over at the empty cubicle in the corner with some satisfaction, and at that moment Matron entered the room with clean linen draped over her arm and advanced towards the unmade bed.

The three girls stared at her in horror.

'Hadn't you better hurry up, girls? The bell will ring in a moment.' Matron's plump person bustled unconcernedly to and fro as she spread clean sheets and put pillows into cases. There was a friendly twinkle of sympathy in her dark eyes as she looked up at the three tragic faces gazing at her. Terry found her voice first.

'Oh, Matron, you aren't going to put anyone else in here?' she implored.

'I'm afraid so,' said Matron firmly. 'I gather you know that Rosemary Lowman is not coming back?'

'Yes. We know. I had a letter this morning. Isn't it sickening?' Terry's voice wobbled a little. 'But why do we have to have someone else in here?' she persisted. 'Surely everyone's fixed up now? Why should anyone want to change?'

'Miss Duncan's orders. New girl. By name Susan Lambert.' Matron plumped up a pillow and set it down again with a little thud.

'A new girl?' Three pairs of eyes again glared at Matron in horror, but she only nodded smilingly and whisked out of the room with a rustle of white, starched apron.

The girls stared at each other dejectedly.

'Well, I call that the limit!' muttered Jennifer savagely. 'It would be bad enough if it were someone we knew. . . .'

'You're right, Tiny. I'm prepared to hate the sight of this—this interloper,' declared Terry disgustedly. 'Aren't you, Dumpling?'

Elizabeth hesitated, her good-natured face thoughtful.

'Well, I'm not pleased, of course; but it's scarcely fair to hate the poor kid in advance, is it? She might be awfully nice—though, of course,' she added hastily, 'she couldn't possibly be quite as nice as Rosemary.

Terry laughed in spite of herself.

'You couldn't hate anyone, could you, Dumpling?' she said affectionately. 'I suppose it is wrong to be prejudiced, but I just hope she's decent, that's all!'

'Hurry up, girls! Didn't you hear the bell?' Fenella

Parsons, the Prefect in charge of their floor, halted in the doorway with a disapproving frown. 'Elizabeth, please close that drawer. Terry, your bedspread is a disgrace. Please straighten it before you leave the room.'

Terry gave the offending bedspread a vicious tweak which did little to improve matters and made a grimace at the Prefect's disappearing back.

'Fenella would do well in the army. She's absolutely wasted here,' Terry affirmed bitterly. She followed the other two slowly and at the door of the dormitory paused and looked back once more at the cubicle in the corner, a bleak feeling of misery flooding over her. The four of them had had such good times together. Now everything was spoiled. Rosemary had left them, and it was only adding insult to injury to remember that tonight her cubicle would be taken over by someone utterly unfamiliar; someone who hadn't even begun the term with them and who knew nothing of Westway's tradition and customs.

Well . . . Terry repeated to herself, I just hope she's decent, that's all!

## 2

## The Substitute

MEANWHILE, the new occupant of Dormitory Ten was on her way to Westways. She sat in the corner seat of the railway carriage, a girl with big hazel eyes and smooth honey-coloured hair, now rather untidily escaping from loosely tied plaits. She was staring hopelessly out of the window, a glum expression on her thin brown face.

The only other occupant of the carriage was a middle-aged lady with a slightly prim look. She was regarding the girl now with a somewhat anxious expression. As the train passed through a small wayside station she consulted her watch and looked happier.

'We shall be there in about a quarter of an hour, Susan. Wouldn't you like to comb your hair, dear? It looks a little untidy.'

Susan Lambert put up an impatient hand and pushed a piece of hair under her hat.

'Oh, it's all right,' she said carelessly.

She turned back to the window, feeling a little guilty about Aunt Jane. Poor darling, it couldn't really have been her fault that Mummy and Daddy had decided to return to Rhodesia alone. At first Susan had been inclined to blame her, for Aunt Jane was Daddy's older sister and a little dictatorial.

Certainly it was Aunt Jane who had said decisively that Westways was the very school for Susan. There they kept their own ponies, the Headmistress was the daughter of an old friend and Devonshire was a beautiful county, said Aunt Jane. In fact she had been so decided about it that, perversely, Susan had been almost glad when she heard the school had no vacancies. Then, last week, there had been a telephone message. One of the pupils was not returning and they could take Susan after all.

Susan couldn't help feeling that Aunt Jane wouldn't be sorry to see her go. After several weeks' stay in England it had been somewhat depressing to realize that, in Aunt Jane's eyes at least, children brought up in Rhodesia had a lot to learn. Susan, on her part, thought ladies and children had a lot to put up with in England. No native servants to fetch and carry for one and pick up the things one dropped. Susan felt she would never get used to it. She sighed heavily and reflected gloomily that things would probably be even worse at school. Again her mind returned resentfully to the old question. *Why* couldn't her parents have taken her back with them? The explanation that her father would have to travel about more now, and that in any case it had been intended for her to go to school in England eventually, failed to convince her that it was anything but an excuse.

The country had grown wilder during the latter part of the journey, and as the small train into which they had changed at the Junction came to a standstill at a wayside station, Susan's spirit's lifted a little. Here, at least, was room to live and breathe. There were few houses to be seen, and there was a long stretch of moor on the skyline. In contrast to the crowded suburban district in which Aunt Jane lived it gave back to Susan a little of the open-air feeling of her life in Rhodesia.

They alighted from the train and went out of the station into a narrow lane. Beyond the close hedges that smelled so sweetly Susan could see the green fields spreading upwards to the rolling hump of brown moor beyond, and the air itself had a spicy tang.

A little farther along the lane stood an old black car, and now an elderly red-faced man of stocky build crossed the road and came towards Susan and her aunt as they stood waiting a little uncertainly.

'For Westways, m'm?' he asked, touching a greying forelock, and picked up Susan's baggage as if it was no more than feather-weight. He stowed it into the back of the car and took the wheel as Aunt Jane and Susan took their seats. They climbed steadily upwards, brushing the hedges so that a shower of drops from the recent rain spattered through the open windows of the car, the road twisting so tortuously that Aunt Jane sat forward in her seat looking a little anxious.

'Isn't this a dreadful road? I hope we don't meet anything coming the other way,' she said nervously.

Susan felt perfectly safe. In front of her the man's thick brown hands held the wheel lightly and confidently, and she was quite sure he had everything under control.

They turned a corner abruptly. Now above the trees at the end of a lane rose the lichen-covered roof and brown chimneys of a big house, and soon they turned in through an open gate and up a widing gravel drive towards it. The car stopped and the man in front came round and opened the door.

'Well, here we are at last, Susan,' Aunt Jane said cheerfully, and tugged at the old-fashioned bell. From the other side of a high laurel hedge Susan could hear girls' voices. They sounded jolly, and for a moment Susan longed to join them. Then she remembered that she was a stranger here and her nervousness swept back.

The door was open now and a rosy-cheeked maid led them across the wide hall to a door marked with the Headmistress's name, saying with a smile:

'Miss Duncan is expecting you. Will you go in, please?'

Susan shrank back behind Aunt Jane. Her imagination had pictured the Headmistress, solid and countrified, with a large stride and a hearty manner, and she had prepared herself to be overwhelmed. When Miss Duncan came towards them, however, she received something of a shock. This tiny, dainty woman with fair, pretty hair and a pink-and-white complexion was as different as possible from the person she had expected. Surely this couldn't be the 'fine horsewoman' Aunt Jane had spoken of? Why, she looked more suitable for afternoon tea in a drawing-room!

Miss Duncan welcomed Susan kindly and asked her a few questions, but most of her conversation was with Aunt Jane about old friends of her mother's, and Susan was able to relax. Presently Aunt Jane prepared to leave as she was anxious to start on the long journey back.

'Good-bye, Susan dear. Be——' For one awful moment Susan thought she would add the word *good,* but, '... Be happy,' finished Aunt Jane instead, and suddenly Susan thought she was really awfully nice, and hated to see her go. She seemed the last link between Susan and her parents, and Susan's panic mounted, though she waved bravely as the old black car drove away again.

Miss Duncan gave her no time, however, for sad thoughts.

'It's quite natural in the circumstances that you should be a little backward, Susan,' she began briskly, 'yet I'd like you to be with girls of your own age. If I put you in the Fourth Form, with opportunities for special coaching, will you work hard and try to catch up?'

It sounded awfully dull, Susan thought, but as she was prepared to hate school anyway it couldn't matter much which form she was in. However, Miss Duncan seemed to be waiting for an answer, so she gave a half-hearted assent with a good deal of mental reserve. Miss Duncan threw her a keen look, and Susan found herself flushing. The Headmistress only paused a moment, then went on in a friendly tone:

'Well, now I must see if I can introduce you to some of your companions. They should be back in a few moments. This is their afternoon for riding.' She hesitated, then said kindly: 'It's always a little hard to be new anywhere, isn't it? But I'm sure you'll soon settle down and like it here.' She slipped a hand under Susan's elbow—she was very little taller than her new pupil—and led her through the wide panelled hall.

Susan looked about her with interest. Westways must surely be a very old place. She liked the wide curved staircase and the minstrel gallery with its carved railing high above at the end of the hall. The sun was shining in through an open door leading into the garden, and as they passed it, Susan heard voices. Miss Duncan paused and looked down the long garden.

'Ah, here they come now,' she remarked. 'These girls are in your form—the Fourth.'

A group of girls in blue blouses and brown jodhpurs came swinging up the path towards them, laughing and chattering. They broke off for a moment at the sight of Susan and stared; then, remembering their manners, murmured, 'Good afternoon.' Miss Duncan propelled Susan forward.

'Girls, this is Susan Lambert, a new pupil. Terry, you'll show her round and make her feel at home, won't you? Susan is in your dormitory. Susan, this is Terry Barton.' With a smile, and a reminder that tea would not be long, Miss Duncan seemed about to leave them. She turned back for a moment, however, and asked, 'What did you make of Cobber this afternoon, Terry?'

'Oh, Miss Duncan, I'm sure he's quite all right now! Masters said no jumping for a while, of course; but he seems quite his old self, and I scarcely noticed his lameness at all.'

Terry's voice was enthusiastic, and Miss Duncan smiled and nodded. As she turned towards her own room and the girls were left alone there was an awkward pause. Terry's feeling of resentment against the newcomer who would take Rosemary's place had renewed itself at the sight of Susan's sulky, withdrawn expression. Then she reminded herself that the girl was probably shy, and held out her hand.

'I ought to say hallo,' she said, with a welcoming smile. 'There isn't much time before tea, but perhaps I can just introduce you to one or two in this menagerie you've joined. This is Jennifer Lee, our nearly six-footer; she gets called Tiny as often as not, and we sometimes wonder if it's cold up there where her head is. This is Pat Hemmings, who has just distinguished herself by falling off the quietest horse in Devonshire——'

'I didn't fall off! Tiny pushed Nigger just as I was dismounting!' protested Pat indignantly, but Terry ignored her and waved her hand again.

'And this is——'

'Thanks, Terry, but I think I'll introduce myself!' laughed Elizabeth, beaming good-naturedly at Susan.

'I prefer my own insults.' She struck a dramatic pose, all the more comical because of her size and the two pronounced dimples she couldn't control. 'I, Susan, was christened Elizabeth Friend. Owing to my somewhat unfortunate *om-bong-pong* (as the French so nicely put it), ignorant and ill-mannered people persist in referring to me as Fatty, or Dumpling. It is a great trial to me. However'—she pulled her mouth down at the corners in mock severity—'I cannot believe, Susan, that you would sink so low.'

Susan did not join in the great gust of laughter which greeted this sally. She stared back at them uncertainly, on the defensive; not quite sure if they were indirectly making fun of her. Elizabeth, noticing her expression, felt uncomfortable, feeling she had blundered. There was a long silence. Then, mercifully, a bell rang just inside the hall, and with a relieved expression Terry dashed forward.

'Great Caesar's ghost! We've only ten minutes to wash and change. Come along, Susan. You'd better come with us. You're in our dorm.'

Susan followed obediently up the stairs and along the corridor to the large airy room she was to share with these three girls.

'There you are. That's your cubicle in the corner. Oh, your bag's there already. Then you're all right.' Terry tried not to remember that it was Rosemary's cubicle that this sulky-looking new girl was taking over, and busied herself with her own toilet.

'Ready?' she asked presently, glancing through the cubicle curtains at Susan's scattered belongings with

24

a little lift of her brows. 'Here——' she began, then thought better of what she was going to say and contented herself with a significant look towards the other two as she led the way downstairs.

In the dining-hall Susan was placed at the end of the Fourth Form table next to the tall girl called Jennifer. She felt very much an alien and made no effort to rouse herself from the gloomy mood she had been in all day. Presently she heard Pat Hemmings remark softly, with a glance at the other end of the table where Terry was deep in a friendly argument with Elizabeth:

'Poor old Terry is pretty fed up about Rosemary, isn't she?'

Jennifer nodded.

'Well, everyone is, but of course it's worst for Terry.' She caught Susan's eye and, feeling that she should be included in the conversation, explained. 'Rosemary was Terry's best friend. She isn't coming back to Westways because she's going to Ireland with her parents. She was in our dormitory and the four of us—Elizabeth, Terry, Rosemary and I—linked our surnames together and called ourselves the Friendleebarlows. We had great fun. Now you've got Rosemary's cubicle.'

There was an uncomfortable pause. Jennifer mentally kicked herself for the tactless wording of her remark but could think of no way to remedy it. Susan stared at her plate with a blank expression.

So it was Rosemary's place she had taken at Westways. Rosemary's parents had been decent enough to take her with them while she, Susan, had been abandoned and deserted. She suddenly hated England and everything in it. She stared moodily out of the window at the garden. The sun had disappeared behind heavy grey clouds, and Susan had a vision of a land of perpetual sunshine with sky a heavenly blue above the trees in blossom and miles of open country broken only by a lonely farm homestead or a rugged pile of rocks. Mummy and Daddy were in Rhodesia without her. Perhaps they were even now riding out to a party at one of the waterholes, or going to tennis or golf, where the native nurse-girls would congregate with their young charges near by. The tears pricked behind Susan's eyelids, and she forgot the times she had called the heat unbearable, the insects which had pestered them and the everlasting mosquitoes. It wasn't fair. No one wanted her. Mummy and Daddy had said they did, but they hadn't yielded to her entreaties to take her with them, and at Westways they were just wishing she was Rosemary.

After tea Susan was kept fully occupied by Matron, who was a little curt about the condition of Susan's cubicle, and satisfying that lady with various details of her past life about which Susan thought she was unnecessarily curious. When prep was over, however, and the other girls were released for the halfhour before bedtime, Susan joined them in the garden. Catching sight of the plump girl who introduced herself as Elizabeth, Susan asked her abruptly:

'Where are the stables?'

Elizabeth cast a longing look towards Terry, who was beckoning her, and shook her head. One must be friendly, especially with a surname like hers to live up to.

'Come along. I'll show you,' she told Susan with a jolly smile.

They went through a white gate into a cobbled yard. The stocky old man who had met them at the station was attending to the horses, helped by a rather stupid-looking lad of about eighteen with a slight limp.

'This is Masters, the head groom, and Tom, who helps him,' said Elizabeth, introducing Susan briefly. Aside, she said to Susan as they moved away: 'Masters has been at Westways for ages. He's a dear, really, though sometimes you might think him a bit of a tyrant.'

Susan remembered the strong brown hands on the wheel and felt she should have known the old man was good with horses. She walked past the two rows of loose boxes. There were sturdy little moorland ponies who looked happy and healthy, and they whinnied a greeting. Besides these there were half a dozen blood ponies and one magnificent cream-coloured hunter which took Susan's eye immediately.

'Beautiful . . . !' she whispered softly, and her expression relaxed as she stroked the animal's velvety coat.

'That's Miss Duncan's Firebrand. He's won a lot of prizes in the showing-class at gymkhanas,' Elizabeth informed her, and Susan had a little feeling of surprise that Westways' tiny and immaculate head-mistress should own such a well-bred and spirited-looking horse. The visit to the stables had cheered her spirits, and she quite forgot her sulkiness in talking to Elizabeth about the merits of the various ponies.

Meanwhile, in the other part of the garden, Terry was asking Jennifer, 'What do you think of the new girl, Tiny?' She looked up at the tall girl beside her with a rather anxious expression.

'Pretty awful.' Jennifer wrinkled her nose comically and grinned. 'What's the matter with her, for goodness' sake? She seems kind of touchy, somehow.'

Terry nodded.

'In a way I'm rather glad to hear you think that. I thought perhaps it was just me.' She sighed heavily. 'Oh, dear, I can't help wishing we didn't have to have her in our dormitory. By the way, *did* you see the way she cast her things about the place? I wondered if I ought to tell her, but I didn't feel she'd take it very well. I guess Matron told her,' she added rather guiltily.

'There goes the bell, and Dumpling has set us a good example by spending all her free time showing Susan round the stables. Here they come now.' Jennifer gave Terry a nudge. 'Come on, we'd better go and meet them. Look cheerful, dearie.'

Terry lagged behind and kicked at a stone dejectedly.

'Can't,' she muttered. 'It's been a *hateful* day.'

## 3

## Pride Goes Before

'SUSAN! Susan! Wake up! You'll have to hurry!'

Susan lifted a tousled head from the pillow and blinked sleepily at Elizabeth who stood beside her bed, shaking her gently.

'Eh? What? Is it . . . time to get up?'

'Yes, of course it is. It's Wednesday. Our morning for grooming; don't you remember?'

Susan dragged herself to a sitting position and yawned dismally. Yes, of course she remembered. Susan had promised herself the night before that she would be up before anyone else, but now that the moment had come she was reluctant to move.

The past few days had been disastrous, with many pitfalls for newcomers unversed in the ways of English school life. As yet Susan had been given no opportunity for making real acquaintance with the stables—the only part of Westways which really interested her. Today, however, it was the turn of the Fourth Form girls to do the grooming and here she was, wasting precious moments.

Making an effort, Susan threw off her tiredness and, climbing out of bed, began to try and make up for lost time.

'But you can't leave your cubicle like that!' Terry said accusingly when Susan, having skimped her toilet, pronounced herself ready to go downstairs with the others.

'I'll do it afterwards,' Susan told her airily. Already she had decided that the other three were inclined to be bossy.

Terry shook her head.

'I've tried to explain to you before that we're all in trouble if you slack, because we lose points for untidy dormitories. We're supposed to keep each other up to standard,' she said a little curtly. Then, relenting, she picked up Susan's pyjamas and began to fold them. 'Come on, you others, we'll do it together for once.' After all, Susan had never had a chance, not with all those little black boys she was always talking about being so ready to clear up after her. 'All the same,' she added warningly, 'don't make the mistake of thinking *we're* always going to be your little black boys!'

The three girls flew about the cubicle efficiently, picking up clothes, shutting drawers and stripping the bed while Susan helped half-heartedly. Ready at last, they went downstairs to find the other members of the Fourth Form already assembled in the lobby where tea and biscuits were being rapidly consumed.

'Come along, you slackers!' Pat Hemmings greeted them gaily. 'I thought you were going to let us do all the work this morning!'

'Rather not. We'll be ready as soon as you are.' Terry grinned good-humouredly and drank tea rapidly to make up for any minutes lost.

'Who is in charge this morning?'

'Jacqueline. It scarcely seems fair that the Head Girl should have to get up early twice a week, does it?'

'Well, why does she have to?' asked Susan curiously.

'There just aren't enough Prefects to go round. Fenella's hopeless about horses, Lesley's practising for her music exam and Hazel has a bad cold,' Elizabeth explained.

'Besides,' put in Pat, 'of all the Prefects, Jacqueline is the best rider, and she's so keen on horses that I don't think she minds. Hazel is quite good, though she's really much more interested in making us play netball and cricket.'

Susan as yet only knew Jacqueline as the fair, pretty girl who read the notices at prayers. She said enviously:

'I suppose the Head Girl can ride whenever she likes?'

Pat looked shocked.

'Good gracious, no! For one thing, she doesn't have much time to herself. She's taking an exam this year, and besides that, there's a lot for her to do as Head Girl. All the same she's awfully good. You should have seen her in last year's gymkhana. She was riding Muffet in the jumping class. She'd never done a clear round before. Jacqueline got wonders out of her.'

'At the riding-school I went to in London I cleared four feet,' Beryl told them importantly.

'After the way you jumped Pegtop on Monday I can scarcely believe it!' laughed Terry.

Beryl hissed angrily.

'Pegtop can't jump for toffee. It wasn't my fault she refused. Was it?' she persisted, watching the expression on Terry's face.

'Well, you did hold her back with too tight a rein, of course. She's used to increasing in the last three strides.' Terry was aware of Beryl's mounting indignation, and not wishing to sound dictatorial, added consolingly: 'I expect it is a bit strange riding in the open field after a school. What about you, Susan? Are you any good at jumping?'

'Yes, I am.' Susan's voice was cool and aloof. She and Beryl had agreed more than once that Terry Barton was far too uppish. Terry, who did not mean to give this impression, was somewhat taken aback by Susan's frigid tone. There was no time for more, however, for just then Jacqueline Graham came tripping down the stairs looking neat and pretty in her blue overall.

'Ready, girls? It's time we were off.'

A moment later the Fourth Form girls, similarly attired in their grooming overalls, set off. Beryl joined Susan and informed her importantly:

'I'm going to have a pony of my own sent down. I've written to Daddy about it.'

'Oh, aren't you lucky!' Susan regarded her enviously. 'Do many of the girls do that?' It would be lovely if she could do the same, but she was sure Daddy would consider it quite unnecessary, and in any case he probably couldn't afford to buy a pony for her.

'No, only a few. Your people have to be really well off, of course. I told Daddy I was sure he would want me to have a decent mount. The School's are just moorland ponies, you see.' Beryl's voice held a note of contempt.

Jacqueline's voice from the rear reproved her sharply.

'Oh, Beryl, don't be such a little snob!' She drew alongside the two younger girls. 'Seriously, you shouldn't speak disparagingly of moorland ponies. They're fine, sturdy creatures, and they know the moors. I've often known them to refuse to go down a track which looked harmless enough, and then, when I've dismounted to find out the reason, discovered a bog or a precipice ahead. Your blood pony will seldom do the same.'

Beryl looked obstinate, but she was sufficiently acclimatized to Westways to realize that when one was in the Fourth one just didn't argue with the Head Girl. Susan, however, was not so wise.

'I've had a lot to do with horses. Blood does tell,' she asserted with a toss of her head.

Jacqueline's eyes flicked over Susan in some surprise.

'Oh yes, I remember. You're the new girl who came from Rhodesia, aren't you?' she said slowly. 'Well, Susan, I agree with you that blood does tell in some ways, but you may be rather surprised yourself at the good performance of some of our moorland ponies. In any case, most of them are quite well-bred too, you know.'

Jacqueline's tone was cool and pleasant. Somehow Susan had the uncomfortable feeling that she had only made herself look foolish. She was glad that they had reached the stables. Masters came towards them with a hearty:

'Good morning, young leddies! Good morning, Miss Jackie.'

'Good morning, Masters,' came the answering chorus.

'He's the only person, besides Miss Duncan, who dares to call her Jackie,' whispered Beryl. 'You see, he knew her in the First Form.'

In a few minutes the girls were busy cleaning the loose boxes, polishing leathers and removing rugs. Susan had been introduced to the chestnut pony named Cobber and told to help Beryl with him. She took an immediate fancy to the pony and spent more time talking to him than she should have done.

'How are you getting on, Susan?' Jacqueline paused beside the younger girl with a smile which faded a little when she saw Susan idling. 'Oh, dear, you haven't done much, have you? Look, Susan, that bridle isn't clean. You've just given it what I'd call "a lick and a promise". You must undo the buckles so that the leather around them gets attention too. You see?' she finished pleasantly.

Susan took the bridle and turned her back with an ungracious mumble.

'Well, I haven't been used to doing this sort of thing. . . .'

'Haven't you? What a pity,' said Jacqueline gravely. 'Well, if you try hard, you'll soon improve.'

Again Susan knew she had got the worst of it. She felt naughtily rebellious, chiefly because Terry, grooming the horse in the loose box next door to her, must have heard the rebuke. Terry had already called her a slacker and now, of course, she would be more uppish than ever.

'In Rhodesia there was always someone to do all the horrid things for me,' she grumbled crossly to Beryl as Jacqueline moved away.

Beryl nodded sympathetically.

'Me too. At least, we haven't any black boys, of course, but the maids do the house and the grooms do the horses.'

Susan gave another half-hearted rub to the bridle she was holding, and then lounged back against the wooden partition dividing the boxes and gave Cobber's glossy chestnut coat a friendly pat.

'Well, anyway, I've done all I'm going to do this morning,' she declared rebelliously. She regarded Cobber speculatively, a glint in her hazel eyes. 'This isn't a bad little pony. I think I'll just try him out on a ride round while I'm waiting,' she said casually.

Beryl's eyes were round and horrified.

'Oh, but you mustn't! I told you before we're not allowed to ride the ponies after grooming. It's very strictly forbidden.'

Susan had made her statement with no serious intention of carrying out her proposal, but now, feeling the challenge of Beryl's horror and realizing that

35

Terry must have been listening, Susan's eyes twinkled wickedly.

'Do you dare me?' she asked, putting her hands on her hips and tilting her head in a provocative attitude. Even then, if Beryl had shown a little tact, she would have been sensible, but Beryl said the very thing to spur Susan on:

'Pooh, it's a dare you'd never take! Besides, Terry is looking at you, Susan. Cobber is one of her special pets, so you'd better be careful.'

'So you think I wouldn't? Well, just watch me, then!' Susan grinned and flung the saddle swiftly across Cobber's back and the bridle over his head, adjusting their straps with nimble fingers. Beryl was really scared and tried to stop her by planting herself in front of the pony. Susan put one foot in the stirrup and swung her leg over.

'Get out of the way, Beryl! You'd better . . .' she threatened.

She urged Cobber forward, and Beryl, still half believing that Susan would not dare to carry out her intention, fell back with a little gasp.

It was fine to be in the saddle again. Susan hadn't really intended to go for a ride, but only to impress Beryl by pretending that she would. Now, however, with the urge to be free again, to feel the air soft and cool across her face in a swift gallop, she gave Cobber's sides a little kick and flicked him gently. Surprised, he moved forward obediently, approving his young rider's expert handling. Susan rode quickly into the field, and now behind her she could hear

Masters' shout and Jacqueline's horrified command, 'Come back at *once*, Susan!'

Pretending not to hear, she rode Cobber forward more urgently. She was in for trouble now almost certainly, and she might as well make it worth her while. Her honey-coloured plaits streamed back from her face as she galloped across the field, taking great gulps of the keen morning air into her lungs. In any case, she would show them all that she could ride. Excitement seized hold of her and she went faster and faster. A wild idea came into her head as she saw a white gate in the fence. She rode Cobber up to it confidently.

'Come on, old boy! Ups-a-daisy!'

She collected him expertly as she urged him at the gate. Cobber loved jumping, and rose gallantly into the air with inches to spare. Susan's breath drew in sharply at the sheer exhilaration of it. Then, as quickly, it was over. As Cobber's feet hit the ground he stumbled. In the split second before they fell, Susan remembered with horror that this, of course, was the pony who had gone lame only a few days before.

Oh, what had she done?

Then she shot over Cobber's head, hitting the ground with a bang, and everything went dark.

## 4

## Consequences

TERRY caught her breath in an angry sob as she ran forward a little ahead of the others. Susan was lying very still, but Terry had eyes only for the chestnut pony, who was now stumbling to his feet and limping badly.

'The idiot! The little idiot!' she muttered. 'Poor Cobber . . . there, my poor darling . . . !'

She seized the pony's rein and soothed its frightened trembling. Masters came panting up to her with Jacqueline and the little group of girls just behind. Jacqueline bent over Susan anxiously. She lifted heavy eyelids and moved painfully.

'I . . . I'm awfully sorry. I didn't mean . . .'

'Don't try to talk and don't move. You might have broken something.' For the life of her, Jacqueline could not keep the stern note out of her voice.

'I'd better carry her in, miss.' Masters dragged his eyes away from Cobber and raised Susan in his strong arms as if she was a baby. 'I'll ask Miss Duncan to ring up the vet and get him to give Cobber a look over. You'll hold him, Miss Terry?'

'Oh, I will . . . !' Terry stroked the pony's head with an agitated hand. 'Oh, I do so hope he's not badly hurt! That girl ought to be——' She closed her lips firmly as Jacqueline stopped her quickly.

'Hush, Terry. That won't help. I'll leave Jennifer with you and perhaps you can take Cobber back to the stables if he seems able to walk. The rest of us will get back to the school.'

'I . . . I think I'm all right now. I can walk, I'm sure . . .' began Susan desperately, but Masters tightened his hold firmly.

'Oh no you don't, miss. Miss Duncan would be sure to say as we ought to take proper precautions.'

The little procession wound through the orchard and across the school garden. One or two girls darted ahead, eager to be the first to take the news back to the school, but Jacqueline stopped them with an authoritative gesture.

'Wait for me, girls, please. I'll go ahead and tell Miss Duncan and please keep calm. We don't want to frighten everyone.'

She hurried forward, and as she entered the building saw Fenella cross the hall. She pounced on her thankfully.

'Oh, Fenella, you're the very person I wanted to see! That new girl, Susan Lambert, rode Cobber at the gate in the field and had a spill. I'm just going in to tell Miss Duncan. Stop the girls from making too much fuss about it, will you?'

'Serious?' Fenella's abrupt manner sometimes came in useful. At least she didn't waste words. Jacqueline, already waiting for an answer to her knock on the door of Miss Duncan's room, matched Fenella for brevity.

'Don't think so. Can't tell yet.'

Then the Headmistress, looking rather surprised at the early summons, opened the door, and Jacqueline went inside while Fenella, with a determinedly fierce expression, prepared to squash any attempt at panic.

'Good morning, Miss Duncan.' Jacqueline hurried through the preliminary and continued as calmly as befitted her position : 'There's been a slight accident. Susan Lambert took Cobber into the field and rode him at the gate just before we finished the grooming. He stumbled as he came down and Susan had a nasty fall. Masters is bringing her in . . . oh, here they are already, I expect.'

'Thank you, Jacqueline. In here, Masters, please.' Miss Duncan had thrown open the door of her sitting-room and now indicated the low divan by the window. She bent over Susan with a concerned expression. 'My dear child . . . !'

'I'm quite all right, Miss Duncan. Really I am. Masters wouldn't let me walk . . .' More shaken than she wanted to admit, Susan suddenly burst into tears. 'I hope . . . I hope . . . Cobber . . .'

'Hush, child! Jacqueline, will you ask Matron to come downstairs and bring a sedative, please? Then telephone for Doctor Clements. Nonsense, Susan, of course we must have the doctor's word that you have no serious injury.'

Susan's protest subsided miserably. She scrubbed at her eyes with a grubby handkerchief and tried to still the trembling of her chin. All this fuss about a little fall! Why, she had been off lots of times. She endured Matron's horrible medicine and the doctor's careful examination with ill-concealed impatience and began to protest all over again when she heard the doctor's pronouncement that she must spend a couple of days in bed.

'No bones broken and no serious damage, but you've had quite a shaking up, young lady,' Doctor Clements told her gruffly, handing her over to Matron, who established Susan in a bed in the sick-room.

Downstairs, the Fourth Form, relieved of their first anxiety, discussed her frankly.

'Spoilt little wretch! She ought to be punished for what she did to Cobber,' Terry said disgustedly. 'Masters says he'll have to have at least two weeks' rest.'

'That will make us short of mounts again,' grumbled Pat.

'Only until my pony comes,' Beryl broke in importantly. 'Dad says he's bought him already and he'll probably be here some time next week. I've just had a letter about it.'

There was a chorus of envious exclamations.

'Oh, Beryl, aren't you lucky!'

'Wish I were you!'

Elizabeth sighed heavily in mock despair.

'Think of poor fat me! I'm so top-heavy on our ponies that I'm always expecting their legs to give way. Now if only my father would send me a nice kind cart-horse! I fancy one with muffs on its feet, for preference.'

A howl of laughter went up at this sally. Terry said severely:

'Of course you feel top-heavy if you will stick to old Meggie. Her legs are so short.'

'No one else likes her.' Elizabeth assumed a pathetic expression. 'Just because she's *fat*, poor dear. I guess we're kindred spirits.'

In the laughter and good-humoured teasing, Beryl lost her moment of triumph and sulked accordingly. All the same, her news was discussed afterwards in private by the occupants of Dormitory Ten.

'It's kind of queer about Beryl,' Terry said reflectively. 'She's always talking about riding, and she's supposed to have done quite a lot at shows with that pony she used to ride at the School, but I don't think she's much good really.'

'I agree. Look at the way she pulls, and then she absolutely muffed the jumping last week,' Jennifer said thoughtfully, while Elizabeth, the charitable, said cheerfully:

'Well, maybe she'll improve a lot when she gets this pony of her own. I say, don't you think we should go up and see Susan?'

Terry looked rebellious.

'Why?' she asked bluntly.

'Well, she's our room-mate, after all.'

'Worse luck. You can go if you like, Dumpling. I shan't.' Terry whistled a tune carelessly. Jennifer looked at Elizabeth.

'Honestly, Dumpling, I don't see why we should. It isn't as if she was at death's door, or anything like that. Matron said she would be about again at the week-end.'

'Oh, well, if you feel like that . . .' Elizabeth's voice trailed away uncomfortably. 'It was only that . . . oh, never mind.'

In the sick-room upstairs Susan lay in bed. She tried to read, but her head ached a little and she had to put the book aside. There seemed nothing to do but think of her troubles and reflect miserably what a bad start she had made at Westways.

Miss Duncan came to see her during the morning and asked her kindly if she was feeling better. She said very little about Susan's disobedience in riding Cobber.

'You did know the rule about it, I suppose, Susan?' was all she asked.

'Yes, Miss Duncan,' mumbled the culprit.

'It's a great pity,' said Miss Duncan gravely, 'because I'm afraid now it will be a full fortnight before you will be able to ride again.'

She didn't say this as if it were a punishment, but Susan couldn't help thinking it hadn't been only the doctor who had fixed the time limit. She wanted to say again that she was sorry, but she couldn't seem to get the words out and after a few minutes, Miss Duncan left her.

By the evening Susan was very bored, and the thought of another long day stretching ahead with no one to talk to seemed intolerable. Why couldn't some of the girls have been in to see her? She supposed Terry was still feeling sore about Cobber. At the thought of Cobber, Susan felt more miserable than ever. She had taken a fancy to the little chestnut pony and would not have caused him pain for the world. Miss Duncan had told her that the vet had said that with rest he would soon be all right again. Susan was terribly thankful that he hadn't permanently injured his leg. It would have been all her fault if he had.

A knock at the door made a welcome break in Susan's thoughts and a moment later Beryl appeared.

'Can I come in?'

'Oh yes, do, please!' Susan's expression brightened. She raised herself on her elbow and indicated the chair by the bed.

Beryl seated herself and said casually:

'Are you all right? You don't look very bad.' Then, taking a letter from her pocket with a flourish, she went on to what, obviously, was the real reason for her visit. 'I had this letter from Daddy this morning. He's bought my pony and it's going to arrive here next week.'

Susan was too glad to see Beryl to be critical. Her eyes sparkled with interest.

'I say, how marvellous for you! I wonder what he will be like. Do you know?'

'Oh yes, he's lovely. Very well bred, and all black with a white star on his forehead.'

'You sound as if you know him already.'

'Well, I feel that I do, in a way, because I asked Daddy at first to buy me the horse I used to have at the riding-school. The man wouldn't sell, although

Daddy offered him more than the pony was really worth. Then Daddy went all over the place, and at last he found one which he says looks exactly like Whisky. I shall call him by that name, too, I think.'

'I suppose your father knows a lot about horses?'

Beryl hesitated.

'Well, no, he doesn't really. But he never minds what he pays, and I know he must have bought a good one. I am looking forward to trying him!'

'I shan't be able to ride for a fortnight,' Susan said gloomily.

'Did Miss Duncan say so? Is that your punishment? We were talking about it downstairs. Terry said——' Beryl stopped and looked primly down her nose. 'But I suppose I ought not to tell you that.'

'What did Terry say? You've got to tell me. Please!'

'Oh, well, you know how keen Terry is on Cobber. She was awfully cross with you because he was hurt, that's all.'

In spite of Susan's persistent questions Beryl refused to say any more, giving Susan the impression that whatever it was that Terry had said had been pretty bad. Now that she had told Susan her own piece of news, Beryl seemed anxious to get away, though Susan did her best to keep her as long as she could. When she had gone, Susan humped herself into a ball and told herself that never, never would she like Westways. If things had been different . . . if Rosemary hadn't left such a gap so that Terry might have liked her . . . Now everyone was against

45

her, and Terry, she was quite sure, hated her. If only she was in Rhodesia with Mummy and Daddy. If only . . . !

And then Matron came in with her supper-tray, and Susan had to blink away the tears and pretend that she wasn't as miserable as she could be. It was difficult . . . pretending.

# 5

## The Arrival of Whisky

SUSAN recovered quickly from the effects of her fall. By the following Monday she was attending classes and feeling quite herself again. It was the day for the Fourth Form's riding-lesson and all the morning Susan brooded over the sad thought that she would not be able to join them. Unable to resist a forlorn hope, she wandered into Matron's room after lunch and protested earnestly that she was absolutely quite all right now.

'Maybe,' agreed Matron cheerfully, 'but if that's a hint that you want to go riding with the others this afternoon, I'm afraid it's no good. You know what Miss Duncan said.'

Susan looked dashed. She wandered towards the door, then turned back with a pleading expression.

'Couldn't you just ask, please, Matron? I . . . I don't like to . . .'

'I'm afraid *I* don't like to either.' Matron laughed a little. 'Cheer up, child, the time will soon pass.'

As Susan still hesitated in the doorway, Miss Duncan entered. She gave Susan a surprised glance, and Susan, though she dare not voice her request, threw all the pleading she could into her expression. Miss Duncan seemed to understand without any words.

'I said Monday *week*, Susan,' she said, shaking her head. Then, relenting a little at the sight of the girl's downcast expression, she added: 'You may go down to the stables to watch the others, if you like. Just a moment . . .' She lifted her hand to check Susan's excited exclamation. 'You will have to give me your promise that you really will not ride this time. I don't want you to rush about either. I shall be out with the girls this afternoon and I don't want to have to worry about what you are doing.'

To Susan this permission was a concession she had scarcely dared to hope for. Her hazel eyes shone.

'Oh, of course I'll promise! Thank you, Miss Duncan.'

Susan slipped away and executed a triumphant little dance along the passage. Nearing her dormitory, however, her feet slowed down and some of her gaiety ebbed away. There had been a noticeable coolness in her welcome back from the sick-room on the previous day. The other two had inquired politely after her health, but only Elizabeth had spoken to her since. It was obvious Terry was still

47

sore about Cobber and that Jennifer had decided to back her up. Probably they would not be at all pleased about her going to the stables, Susan thought bitterly.

During Susan's brief absence in Matron's room, however, Elizabeth had been lecturing the other two severely.

'I think you two are being awfully mean about Susan,' she scolded. 'I guess she's felt pretty strange and miserable right away from the life she's been used to. After all, the kid's been punished enough, hasn't she? Need you rub it in quite so hard!'

Terry's sense of fair play made her realize the justice of the accusation, though characteristically she had to defend herself.

'Maybe you're right, Dumpling. I haven't such a sweet nature as you have, but . . . oh, well, I will try to be nicer. You know how it is. I've missed Rosemary so much and it seems extra hard to have to sort of put up with Susan instead.'

It was this last sentence that Susan, walking slowly along the corridor, overheard. She halted in the open doorway, her breath coming quickly and her face very red and angry.

'It wasn't my fault that Rosemary didn't come back! Goodness knows,' she gulped a little, then went on fiercely: 'I never wanted to come to this school in the first place. I knew it would be hateful, and it is!'

Elizabeth and Jennifer glanced at Terry appealingly. She was looking very uncomfortable.

48

'Honestly, Susan——' she began.

Susan flung up her head defiantly.

'Oh, don't bother to make excuses. I know you've disliked me from the beginning, and especially since I rode Cobber.' Her voice took on a sarcastic note as she continued: 'You'll be delighted, I'm sure, to know that Miss Duncan says I can go down to the stables to watch you this afternoon. Anyway, even if you're not, you'll have to put up with me just the same.'

Terry took a step forward.

'I'm sorry you heard me say that about putting up with you, Susan,' she said earnestly. 'I didn't really mean it just as it must have sounded. Perhaps I have been in rather a bad mood because I'm upset about Rosemary not coming back and I ought not to take it out on you. Oh, dear, it's dreadfully difficult to explain; but please believe that I'm really glad you can come with us this afternoon, Susan.'

For a moment Susan did believe her. Then her eyes fell on the three pairs of jodhs laid out ready to wear. What was the good of going down to the stables if she couldn't ride?

'I don't think I want to come anyway,' she muttered, and going over to her cubicle pulled the curtains to with a clatter.

Terry shrugged her shoulders and, making a little grimace at Elizabeth, went into her own cubicle. The silence continued while the three girls dashed into their jodhs and blue blouses. Then, at the last

49

moment, Elizabeth popped a smiling face into the corner cubicle and said cheerfully:

'We're ready, Susan! Oh, come on, kid, don't be stuffy. It will be more fun than staying indoors on a lovely day like this. Cheer up! Next week you'll be riding with us instead of watching us.'

Elizabeth's jolly grin was always infectious. Susan's expression relaxed a little and, smiling faintly, she allowed herself to be argued out of her decision to remain at school and was presently hurrying after the others.

Down at the stables Masters was waiting for them. It was the first time Susan had seen him since the day of her fall, and she flushed a little as she saw his eyes fixed on her with a grave expression. When he asked her how she was feeling, she wished they could have been alone so that she could explain to the old man that she hadn't meant to hurt Cobber. Then she heard Beryl beside her exclaim:

'Oh, Masters, *when* do you think my pony will arrive?'

'He has arrived. He came last night.' This information, given in Masters' dry voice, sent Beryl into a transport of excitement.

'He has? Oh, Masters, no one told me! What is he like? How did he travel? Can I ride him now?'

'All them questions to be answered at once, I suppose? Well, Miss Beryl, he's quite a good little pony. A bit spirited and he hasn't been too well trained, I imagine, though he travelled well. Yes, I suppose you can try him out.' Masters jerked a thumb in the direction of the new pony's loose box and Beryl dashed away excitedly, dragging Susan after her. She opened the door of the box where a pony with a white star on his forehead was casting a restless eye at the newcomers and shaking his head impatiently.

'Oh, he's beautiful, isn't he, Susan? And he's exactly like the other Whisky, as Daddy said. Hey, Whisky, my pretty, I'm your new mistress!' Beryl put out an impetuous hand to fondle the pony's ears. He turned his head with such an abrupt movement that she drew her hand away again, startled.

'He almost bit me!' she said indignantly. 'I hope he's not vicious!'

'You shouldn't touch his head first. Some horses are inclined to be a bit touchy about that if they don't know you,' reproved Susan. 'You ought to just speak to him quietly and then pat his back.'

Beryl tossed her head.

'The other Whisky loved me to stroke his ears,' she said aggrievedly. She lifted down the new bridle which hung on the wall at the back of Whisky's box. Masters came behind her and put a restraining hand on her arm.

'Just a moment, Miss Beryl. I want to see to the other young leddies first. That pony ain't used to you yet. Everything's strange, and he wants handling gently.'

Beryl pouted and threw Susan a rebellious look as Masters moved away again. Susan grinned at her a little wickedly.

'Better wait, hadn't you?' she advised. 'You don't want to be forbidden to ride, like me, do you?'

'That was different. This is the proper time for riding and I'm sure I could deal with Whisky all right,' Beryl said, with a superior air. 'Still, I suppose I had better wait for Masters. Oh, gracious, a good thing I did! Here's Miss Duncan coming.'

Susan turned her head curiously, Miss Duncan, clad in the smartest and trimmest of riding-costumes, was just coming through the gate towards them. Calling a word to Masters, she went to Firebrand's loose box and a few moments later rode him out into the field where now the rest of the girls, already mounted, were waiting for her. It had seemed to Susan that Firebrand, though a lovely creature, must be almost too big for Miss Duncan. Now, seeing them together, she realized that she had been wrong and the two were perfectly in tune. Miss Duncan had a perfectly balanced seat, and as she moved across the field, Susan felt she knew what people really meant when they described a good rider as being 'part of his horse'.

'She looks fine, doesn't she?' Susan watched them all ride off together with an envious sigh.

'Who? Oh, Miss Duncan . . . ? She's won heaps of cups.' Beryl was too interested in her new pony to be more than casual. Under the expert eye of Masters, Whisky was saddled and Susan noticed with some amusement that his new bridle was equipped with what her father used to call contemptuously 'all the bits and pieces'. Then Beryl, mounted at last, called to her excitedly:

'Look, Susan, isn't he a little beauty!'

Since his arrival Whisky had been resting and was obviously very fresh. Perhaps he thought he would prove the strange young rider on his back and teach her a lesson for hurting his mouth with her hard hands. At any rate, when Masters let him go he rolled his eyes and bucked, pretending to be very fierce. Beryl looked a little scared as she did her best to subdue him. She knew Susan was watching her and wanted to show off. Disregarding Masters' warning not to pull so hard, she pulled even harder and gave Whisky a sharp flick with her crop. Surprised and cross, the pony bucked again. Beryl lost her stirrups and, had it not been for Masters' helping hand, would have fallen off. Almost crying with annoyance, she had to endure the groom's corrections, 'Just as if,' as she said to Susan afterwards, 'I haven't been riding for ages!'

Susan, watching, decided that Beryl didn't know the first thing about riding and, feeling that she was making a bad matter worse, went over to the other side of the stable to visit Cobber. Stroking his glossy head gently, she murmured to him:

'Have you forgiven me, old boy? You know I wouldn't have hurt you for the world, don't you?'

Fishing in her pocket, Susan brought out a couple of well-covered apple cores she had been saving for the pony as a peace-offering. Cobber nuzzled his soft nose into her hand and munched them gratefully. Susan put her arm around his neck and hugged him gently.

'I knew you'd forgive me, Cobber darling. You're a grand little jumper, and another day we'll have some more fun, won't we?'

All the riders were out of sight now, even Masters and Beryl. It wasn't much fun hanging about waiting for the others to come back, thought Susan, feeling lonely and a little cross. She wandered about, and presently went along the side of the hedge into the next field. It was a very warm day, almost like summer, and Susan threw herself down on the grass and wondered rather wistfully what her mother and father were doing at that moment. Were they missing her? The thought transported her far away to Rhodesia, and she returned to her surroundings with a little start, realizing suddenly that a hum of voices of which she had only subconsciously been aware was coming nearer. Someone sounded very angry. Susan thought she caught the words, 'You'll do as I say!' before she realized that whoever it was seemed unaware of her presence and she should not be listening.

Susan scrambled to her feet. Through a gap in the hedge she could see a man of about sixty with a low forehead and small bloodshot eyes. His companion was younger and, as the two men turned their heads towards her, Susan saw that it was Tom, the stable-boy. His freckled face was deeply flushed and his mouth hung open in startled surprise, but the older man looked quite composed. He laughed a little.

'I was just asking this young man here if he has seen a sheep. I suppose you haven't, miss?'

Susan stared.

'A . . . a sheep?' she repeated stupidly.

'Yes, a sheep, miss. Don't you know what one looks like?' the man jeered. 'Lost a sheep, I have. Been hunting hours for her. Sure you ain't seen her, either of you?'

Embarrassed, Susan shook her head. It was so silly when she knew perfectly well that the man had been arguing fiercely with Tom only a few moments before. Tom was already stomping across the field, his back solidly towards her. There seemed nothing else to say. The man gave another short laugh and, turning, Susan hurried across the field. With relief she saw that the riders were now coming back across the moor and ran towards them, forgetting the little incident almost at once. She could see Beryl on the black pony with the white star. She was trotting along in quite good style, Masters by her side. They had evidently met the others on the way back.

As she drew nearer, Susan saw that Whisky looked ill at ease and Beryl's expression seemed a little tense. These two made a sharp contrast to Miss Duncan who now, on the big cream-coloured hunter, appeared over the brow of the hill where the fields met the spreading moors. Horse and rider moved as one as they galloped across the cropped turf. Susan watched them enviously. Then Terry passed her, waving her crop in a gay greeting, and completely at ease on the brown pony called Dallas.

Next week . . . next week . . . thought Susan almost despairingly. It seemed such a long time to wait.

# 6

## Prep with a Difference

SUSAN came slowly across the garden, trying not to mind that the other girls were chattering and laughing together in gay groups, making no effort to include her. Somewhat against her will she had been playing netball with a mixed team drawn from the Third and Fourth Forms. Resisting Hazel's enthusiastic efforts to rouse her, Susan had played in a half-hearted way, thinking rebelliously all the time that this was a poor substitute for riding. Why couldn't they choose what they did with time not spent at actual lessons?

Surprisingly, the other girls had seemed to resent her lack of enthusiasm, and now she was alone.

'Miss Duncan wants you, Susan.'

Jacqueline's quiet voice cut sharply across Susan's preoccupation, banishing all other thoughts. What could be the reason for this summons to the Headmistress's presence? Was she in trouble again? She hovered nervously just inside the door of Miss Duncan's room a few minutes later.

'Sit down, Susan, will you?' Miss Duncan pushed a pile of letters aside and smiled across her desk at Susan. Then she went on abruptly, 'You're not keeping up very well with the work of the Fourth Form, are you, Susan?'

Susan looked down at her hands. The answer seemed too obvious, but Miss Duncan was apparently waiting for a reply, so she supposed she had to say *something*.

'It's very hard . . .' she mumbled.

'And you've tried?'

Susan flushed. Lifting her head she stared somewhat defiantly into the cool grey eyes facing her.

'Yes . . .' she began, then her eyes fell again. 'Well . . .'

'That's just what I thought.' The Headmistress nodded pleasantly. There was a long pause. She went on quietly, 'So you'd like to be put down into the Third Form instead?'

Susan hesitated. Her imagination swiftly mustered the whole of the Third Form for review. There was no one she would want to be friendly with. Sheila Clark was rather nice, but she was much younger. In the Fourth Form were Terry, Elizabeth, Jennifer, Pat, Beryl. . . . She realized with some surprise that she would miss them all if she had to leave them.

'Do I have to?' she asked desperately.

'Certainly you have to unless you can really make

up your mind to do better. Personally, I think you could catch up, but the decision is with you, Susan. Will you make the effort or will you take the line of least resistance and join the Thirds?'

Susan scarcely hesitated. In the Third Form the work would be much easier, of course; but, apart from leaving the others, how humiliating her fall would be! She set her mouth firmly.

'I'd like you to give me another chance, please, Miss Duncan.'

'Good. I hoped you would say that. I realize that it is not your fault that you are rather backward in certain subjects, but you have a good brain, and if you try hard I think you will soon find things easier. We, on our side, will do our best to help you. Now although the coaching you are already having with Miss Carr and Miss Walsh is useful, they have not a great deal of time to spare, and in any case you must have your free time, too. A suggestion has been made which I think will help a lot. . . .'

'Yes?' prompted Susan hopefully.

'Well, as you probably know, I always talk over my problems with the Sixth Form, and they put forward any ideas they may have. Fenella has kindly said that she is willing for you to do your prep in her study twice a week. She will be working too, but she will be ready to answer any questions or make any point clear which you do not understand.'

Susan's face fell. How awful to have to study with Fenella, the sergeant-major; the Prefect for whom no one ever did anything quite right and in whom no one ever saw the slightest sign of a softer side! Susan couldn't understand Fenella making the offer, but she was quite sure that it would be unbearable to be condemned to the Prefect's exclusive company twice a week. Miss Duncan, however, gave Susan no chance to protest. She rose now from her desk as if to indicate that the interview was at an end and said firmly:

'Well, that's settled, then. Tuesdays and Thursdays. You can begin this evening, and you'll do your best to take every advantage of Fenella's kind offer, won't you?'

'I——' began Susan; but Miss Duncan took a piece of paper from her desk and, folding it, handed it to Susan with a smile.

'Take this list to Matron, will you? And hurry along now, dear, or you will be late for tea.'

Susan sighed heavily as she went along the passage to Matron's room. Tuesdays and Thursdays . . . oh, dear! How would she ever bear it? And this very evening she would have to face the ordeal in Fenella's study for a whole hour! In spite of the clanging summons of the tea-bell downstairs, Susan lingered for a moment in Matron's comfortable and homely presence.

'Something on your mind?' inquired Matron, raising her eyes from the list in her hand and peering over her glasses at Susan.

'Not . . . exactly. . . .' Susan traced a finger thoughtfully round a panel of the door, and went on in a burst of confidence, 'I'm going to do prep in Fenella's room twice a week. . . .'

'H'm. And you don't like the idea of that much, I can see. Well, Susan, you must remember that sometimes one has to dig very deep for gold. Now run along, child, or you won't get any tea.'

You have to dig very deep for gold . . . what had Matron meant by that remark? Did she mean that one had to try hard if one wanted to gain knowledge? Well, of course she didn't want to be backward and she liked learning things even if she had, perhaps, been a little lazy lately. But to dig . . . with Fenella. . . . It sounded awfully dull. And how could she, particularly, be expected to have a thing in common with Fenella who—quite surprisingly at Westways—didn't even like riding and horses!

Susan slipped into her place at the Fourth Form's table. The others were talking excitedly and scarcely seemed to notice her arrival. At first she paid little attention to their conversation.

'. . . well, the notice was on the board just before tea.'

'What was the date?'

'July twenty-third. You know we really ought to begin training right away. We've had almost no practice with jumping this term.'

'Well, Masters and Tom have been making some new jumps and they're only just finished.'

Susan's interest was aroused at last.

'What are you talking about?' she asked eagerly.

Beryl, who was always ready to inform others, told her importantly:

'Why, the Gymkhana, of course.'

'What Gymkhana?'

'Of course, you don't know about it——'

'We have it at the end of the summer term——'

'Proceeds in aid of the hospital. It's great fun——'

'There are showing-classes and jumping-classes. And all the usual things like musical chairs and bending. . . .'

They all talked at once, the words tumbling over each other. Evidently the Gymkhana was a most exciting event. Susan's eyes sparkled. Why hadn't she heard about this before? She had a vision of herself excelling in every event. Then her face fell. She had no pony of her own, so how could she?

'How do you arrange it?' she asked anxiously. 'I don't see how you sort out the school ponies. I mean, how do you decide who rides them?'

'Oh, there's a committee,' Pat informed her. 'Miss Duncan, of course, one or two of the mistresses and some outsiders. We have heats beforehand, taking turns in the events with the horses we fancy, and the Committee chooses the best to represent the School. We throw some of the events open to outsiders, you see, so we have to put up a good show.'

'No one is allowed to compete in more than two events, in any case,' Elizabeth explained.

'Except those with their own ponies, surely?' Beryl put in possessively.

Terry frowned.

'I don't know that there is any rule about that, but so far those with their own ponies have kept to the same as the others and lent their mounts out to their friends,' she said severely. 'Even Hazel didn't ride Lady Jane for more than the two events.'

'Surely I don't have to lend Whisky if I don't want to?' Beryl said sulkily, then noticing the other girls' disgusted expressions, she added apologetically: 'I mean, I'm only just getting him used to me. I think it would be bad for him to have another rider yet.'

'Please yourself, of course.' Terry turned away and began a conversation with Pat about something else. They were all getting a little tired of Beryl and her pony.

Tea over, Susan had to turn her mind from the pleasant subject of the Gymkhana to the immediate and not-so-pleasant prospect of the evening ahead. She made her way slowly towards Fenella's study, wishing she could get out of it. It didn't make matters easier to remember the horrified sympathy of the other girls when they heard of the new idea. Some even regarded it as a kind of punishment and wanted to know what Susan had done *now*.

So it was with a sinking heart that Susan knocked on the door of Fenella's room. The brusque tone of the Prefect's voice as she told Susan to come in did nothing to dispel the younger girl's gloom, and the corners of her mouth were turned down in a miserable expression as she arranged her books on the small table just behind Fenella's desk.

'Cheer up,' said Fenella suddenly. 'I shan't eat you.'

Susan, startled, turned her head sharply and caught an amused gleam in Fenella's eye. She smiled faintly. Then, before she could think of anything to say, the gleam had gone and Fenella's head was bent over her books with an absorption which seemed to forbid further talk. Susan opened her Arithmetic and settled down to her preparation, determined not to ask Fenella anything at all.

The first sum went well. Susan drew a line triumphantly below the answer and felt pleased with herself. The next question presented a knotty problem, however. If six trucks, each carrying a ton and a half of coal . . . It was terribly complicated. Susan's mind began to revolve as if the trucks, the men, the weight and the time were using it as a perpetual merry-go-round and the whole thing seemed hopeless. This was, of course, the occasion when she should ask for Fenella's help; but Fenella was apparently oblivious to her surroundings, her back bent in a hump over her books in an attitude of concentration.

Susan decided afterwards that Fenella must have eyes in the back of her head, for suddenly she turned and said, so abruply that Susan jumped :

'Bring the book here, Susan. We'll have a go at that together.'

Susan proferred the book with a hopeless gesture. It seemed as impossible to expect anyone to explain that question so that she could understand it, as it would be to hack one's way out of a jungle with a penknife. Then Fenella began to talk.

At first Susan had the curious feeling that she was separated from the explanation and away in a little world of her own where nothing could penetrate.

Then suddenly she began to see what Fenella meant. The trucks, the men, the weight and the time ceased to go round and round in her mind confusedly and sorted themselves out, each into its own rightful position.

'Why, of course . . .! It's easy, isn't it?' she exclaimed eagerly. 'I was all muddled up, but now I can see it quite clearly.'

Fenella nodded gravely.

'Of course it's easy, if you keep your head. Next time don't get into such a panic.'

She turned abruptly to her own books again, but not before Susan had caught a glimpse of that amused gleam again. She went back to her table, feeling much happier. It was going to be all right after all. Perhaps they had all been wrong about Fenella. Anyway, even if Fenella didn't like horses and ordered people about in a voice like a sergeant-major's, Susan felt that she would never be so scared of her again. She remembered what Matron had said. Was that what she meant after all? Could Fenella . . . be gold?

Maybe.

# 7

## Trouble Over Cobber

'I REALLY shan't be able to wear these jodhs of mine much longer.' Jennifer looked down at her long legs with a pained expression. 'Honestly, I don't know what Mummy will say if I write home to say I want *another* pair!'

'Poor old Tiny!' Terry commiserated mockingly. 'She reminds me of Alice in Wonderland. You know . . . "Good-bye, feet!"'

The others shrieked with laughter, and Jennifer's expression became more pathetic than ever.

'It's all very well to make fun of me,' she protested. 'You others don't know what a trial it is to grow as I do. Honestly, I can't bend properly in these trousers because the seat comes in the wrong place!'

'Try cutting up the seams of the legs so that you can pull them up higher,' suggested Susan helpfully.

'Then they won't meet my shoes, and I'll look like Little Lord Fauntleroy in knee-breeches. No, I'll have to write to Mummy. Perhaps I could sell these. You don't think anyone here might buy them from me?' Jennifer brightened at the idea.

Elizabeth shook her head.

'Sorry, dearie. I'm afraid you didn't improve the second-hand value when you sat on that wet fence,' she teased.

Jennifer turned her long neck and twisted herself round as far as she could in an effort to survey the damage.

'Oh, that . . . ? A touch of petrol is all that is required,' she said airily.

'Oh, come on, girls,' Terry urged impatiently. 'This is no time for a sartorial discussion. Posh word . . . !' She grinned and pushed Susan ahead of her out of the door. 'If that lanky wretch has made us late . . . !' she threatened darkly.

Susan took the stairs two at a time, her spirits high. Everything had been much nicer lately, and it was good to find Terry and the others including her in the teasing and fun that went on in Dormitory Ten. It gave her a new and satisfactory feeling of belonging. In addition to this it was the Fourth Form's day for riding—always a welcome event—and to crown it all they were today going to practise jumping for the first time since she had come to Westways.

Going down to the stables, Susan tried to keep with the other three and avoid Beryl, who was looking sulky. But Beryl refused to be avoided.

'Susan, do walk with me,' she pleaded, and Susan halted, irresolute. A moment later she was sorry that she had done so, for Beryl had a grievance and continued: 'Don't you think it's unfair? I went down to see Whisky this morning, and Masters says I have to take him over the sacks this afternoon instead of the proper jumps.'

'I expect he only wants to make quite sure that you can jump Whisky,' Susan consoled her. 'When you have done the sacks you can go on to the jumps.'

Beryl's face was stormy. She kicked a stone viciously with her foot, and in spite of the fact that it went sideways and caught Susan on the shin she omitted to apologize.

'I'm sure I don't know why, but Masters seems to make out that Whisky is badly trained. As if he could be, after all the money Daddy paid for him! He wants me to start right at the beginning again and take him forward slowly. I'm sure Whisky is all right. Masters doesn't know what he's talking about.'

Susan looked shocked.

'Oh, Beryl! Masters has been riding for years and years! Terry says he has won hundreds of cups.'

'*Terry* . . . !' muttered Beryl bitterly. '*Terry* this and *Terry* that . . . ! I suppose now you've been taken up by that lot you've no time for *me*.'

'Oh, don't be silly!' In spite of her protest, Susan felt that there was something in what Beryl had said. It was true that she hadn't liked to be with Beryl so much lately. Perhaps it was because she always managed to find something to grumble at while the others were funny and jolly. Mercifully she was spared further comment by their arrival at the stables where Beryl left Susan immediately and, going to Whisky's box, began to saddle him.

The others dispersed to the various boxes. There was rarely any trouble about sharing the ponies. Masters insisted on them changing round for grooming so that they should get used to them all, but when it came to riding, the girls had their favourites and it was tacitly expected that, once chosen, they would keep to them unless there was some special reason.

Susan made straight for Cobber. For the first time he had been pronounced fit for riding and jumping and she was looking forward to putting him through his paces. It was therefore something of a shock to find Terry heading in the same direction.

'Oh, but, Terry, I'm riding Cobber,' she said, her anxiety making her tone brusque.

'Sorry, but I am,' Terry contradicted her lightly.

'But why? Dallas is your special, surely?'

Terry hesitated. Admittedly she had been riding Dallas regularly lately, but she had also been watching for Cobber's full recovery as anxiously as Susan. It seemed difficult to explain that she and Rosemary had a mutual arrangement by which they took Dallas and Cobber alternately and that she considered both the ponies her specials. Perhaps she had not quite forgiven Susan for laming Cobber again. At any rate, remembering it again, Terry suddenly couldn't bear the idea of her monopolizing him. Dallas was a darling, but . . . so was Cobber. She and Rosemary had never been able to decide which of the ponies they liked best, and that was why they had shared them. Elbowing Susan out of her way, Terry took down Cobber's saddle.

'You can have Dallas today,' she said shortly. 'I'm going to ride Cobber.'

'You're not! I'm going to!' Susan faced Terry

**68**

angrily across Cobber's broad back. 'Why should you decide?'

The two girls glared at each other fiercely; Terry quite forgetting that earlier that afternoon she had decided that Susan wasn't at all a bad kid, after all; Susan ignoring the fact that only a few moments ago she had been proud of Terry's friendliness. Both were quite determined not to give way. Then Masters strolled across to them.

'Eh now, what's all this, young leddies?' he asked, in his slow drawling way. 'Miss Terry, I thought you would be riding Dallas again this afternoon?'

Terry threw up her head defiantly and stared at him.

'I'm riding Cobber,' she stated flatly.

If there had been a chance of her having her own way before, Terry should have known that by her attitude it was doomed. Up at Westways, Miss Duncan had the ruling, but Masters considered the stables his own kingdom and brooked no interference with his ruling. Now his red-brown eyes held a fiery gleam.

'Miss Susan will ride Cobber,' he said quietly. Somehow Terry found herself giving way. With a final glare at Susan she walked across to Dallas' box. Masters followed her. He knew how much Terry loved the ponies and had perhaps something of an inkling of what lay behind her attitude. He said softly: 'Don't worry, Miss Terry. Miss Susan's a good rider all right, and the little chap knows it too.'

Terry knew when she was beaten, but she couldn't feel pleased about it.

'All right,' she said shortly. As she threw the saddle across Dallas' back she whistled a gay tune so that no one would think she minded terribly.

Susan's fingers shook a little as she fastened the buckles on Cobber's bridle. If only it hadn't happened! Now she half wished she had given in, for perhaps Terry would be against her again. In spite of the thought, Susan's spirits rose as she rode Cobber out into the field and saw the jumps which Masters and Tom had made look quite professional. There was a brush fence, a double-bar which could be made into a triple when necessary, an 'in and out' and a most realistic wall. Well to the side of the field had been placed sacks, well filled with straw, for the beginners, and to these Masters now beckoned Susan.

'I've not actually seen you jump yet, miss,' he said, with a grin. 'I know you cleared the gate somehow, but I missed seeing it. I'd like to watch your style in something a little less dangerous, please.'

Susan grinned and, leaning over Cobber's glossy neck, patted him as she rode him forward.

'Kid stuff,' she told him softly. 'But do it nicely, old boy.'

She rode him quietly at a canter towards the sacks, but when she collected him for the low jump he shied and ran around it. Three times Susan tried, showing no impatience. Still he refused. Masters watched with a grim expression on his weather-beaten face. Susan threw him a desperate glance.

'Scared,' was the old man's terse pronouncement.

Susan bit her lip. No doubt Terry was watching

70

too. Was she perhaps thinking that Cobber would do the jump for her? Slowly Susan slipped from the saddle and held out the reins to Terry.

'You try,' she said curtly.

Terry tossed her head.

'No, thanks!'

'Please!'

Terry hesitated. Then she threw Dallas' reins across to Susan and, mounting Cobber, rode him forward. Three times Terry tried to make him jump, but each attempt ended in failure.

'You've spoilt him,' she said bitterly as she handed the reins back to Susan. Susan threw up her head defiantly but there was desperation in her eyes.

'Patience, Miss Susan,' Masters said softly. 'You're going to need a lot of it if you want to cure him. He's just scared and you've got to win his confidence back.'

Susan threw him a grateful look.

'Oh, Masters, I'll try hard!'

The old man nodded and turned away, calling to Beryl who, trying with little success to make Whisky sit still, looked flustered and cross.

'Now, Miss Beryl, let's see what you can do.'

Exasperated with her restive mount, Beryl gave him a sharp flick with her crop and rode him towards the sacks. Whisky tossed his head and, cantering forward, stopped abruptly, refusing the low jump. The second time he took it, but rather too quickly for Beryl, who looked a little nervous as she rode back to the others. She tried to hide it with a laugh.

'Fresh, isn't he? I expect he thinks silly little jumps like that aren't worth bothering about. The man Daddy bought him from said he can clear four feet quite easily!'

'No doubt.' Masters nodded gravely. 'But here he'll have to learn to behave properly over a low jump before he goes on to the others. Now, keep your hands down, Miss Beryl, and don't pull on the reins just as he is in position. Now, off you go again.'

'Must I? But he did that easily!' Beryl began to protest again, but Masters was adamant and she had to give in, though she looked very sulky about it.

Meanwhile, Susan decided to give Cobber a rest from the sight of the sacks and joined the riders on the other side of the field. Masters had told them to wait until he was free to watch them at the jumps, so they were practising changing legs and cantering figures of eight. Susan couldn't help smiling a little at the sight of the plump Elizabeth on the equally plump pony called Meggie, but she had to admit she managed her well. Jennifer, too, was doing well on Nigger.

'I do wish Masters would hurry up,' Pat was remarking as Susan came up. She was riding Pegtop, a small grey pony who had just changed legs with surprising agility. 'Pegtop is pretty good, don't you think?' she asked Susan.

'Listen to her talking!' scoffed Terry, making a neat turn on Dallas. 'No one could make a mistake with Pegtop. She always behaves herself, whoever rides her. Now Dallas——' She stopped abruptly as the pony bucked playfully and had to give him all her attention so that Pat finished the sentence for her with a grin:

'Yes, Dallas needs riding, I can see!'

Susan tried Cobber in a figure of eight, and was just completing it, none too successfuly, when Beryl rode over to them, Masters running along by her side.

'All right now, young leddies. I'll see you all take the brush in turn. Miss Terry, will you go first, please?'

Dallas, Pegtop, Nigger and Muffet went over well. Several girls had two or three refusals from their ponies and some only just scraped over in bad style. Then Masters took separately those who had refusals and those who had jumped badly while the others went back to their schooling.

Beryl had not been allowed to jump. She muttered fiercely to Susan:

'I'm not going over the sacks again, although Masters said I was to go on practising. I know Whisky thinks they're potty. I can't think why Masters won't let me jump properly.'

'But, Beryl, if you satisfy him he will. You know the girls say Masters never alters his mind, ever. Come on, I'll come over there with you. Don't forget Cobber has refused altogether.'

'Oh, well, I don't suppose he'll ever jump again now,' Beryl said carelessly, and did not see the bleak look which came over Susan's face. They tried the

73

novices' jump again. This time Whisky behaved beautifully, as even Masters admitted when at last he was induced to look. Cobber, however, put his ears flat against his head and refused to jump at all.

'Can I try the brush now?' asked Beryl eagerly.

Masters pulled his great silver watch out of his pocket and consulted it solemnly.

'Sorry, miss, No time left now. Next time I'll take you first.'

'Well . . . !' began Beryl wrathfully, as Masters strode away. Susan saw that if she was not careful Beryl would be pouring out her grievances again in another moment. She spurred Cobber forward and rode towards the stables, avoiding her. She wasn't in the mood to hear Beryl's troubles, for she had plenty of her own.

Susan had been looking forward with eagerness to the afternoon, but now it was over and it had not been a success as far as she was concerned. Cobber wouldn't jump any more, and it was all her own fault. What was more, everyone knew it and was probably talking about her behind her back. And things were as bad as ever between she and Terry after their quarrel about Cobber, she supposed.

Susan sighed and taking Cobber to his box rubbed him down and made him comfortable. Next door to her Terry was occupied with Dallas. She ignored Susan completely, and ran off when she had finished to link up with Jennifer and Elizabeth as they crossed the garden. Susan followed slowly. There was a look of determination on her face. She wouldn't be beaten if she could help it. She was going to get Cobber back into his old form somehow.

Then she would show Terry . . . !

## 8

### Leads to a Quarrel

I F Fenella hadn't exactly become a friend, at least she was no longer an enemy, and between Susan and the Sixth-Former there had developed an easiness in working together. Although Fenella jumped on Susan for her misdemeanours just as much as she did on the others, she was most helpful and friendly during the hour they were shut up in the study together. So much so that Susan found herself taking a new interest in her lessons.

'You explain things so well, Fenella. You ought to be a teacher,' she said that evening, as she packed up her books and prepared to leave.

Fenella, surprisingly, blushed.

'I might be . . .' she said hesitantly. Then, rather fiercely, 'And I suppose you think I look like one, eh?'

Susan's eyes travelled swiftly over Fenella, and it was her turn to blush. As a matter of fact, now that she thought about it, Fenella did look a little like the proverbial schoolmarm with her straight dark hair pulled tightly back from her too-high forehead. Her heavy-rimmed eyeglasses seemed to dominate her face, and her mouth wore an habitually severe expression.

'Go on, say it!' Fenella almost barked the words.

'Well . . .' Susan faltered, then plunged on desperately: 'Well, lots of teachers are awfully nice-looking, I mean, there's Miss Clark and Miss Walsh. They don't look a bit like schoolmistresses.'

'But you think *I* do, don't you?'

Fenella pushed away the knowledge that to a Sixth-Form girl it shouldn't matter what a Fourth-Former thought, in any case. She also knew the answer to her question, but somehow felt she must hear Susan say it.

'Well . . .' began Susan, again rather miserably. She didn't want to offend Fenella, but it seemed impossible to prevaricate. She threw caution to the winds and went on defiantly: 'Yes, you do, then, if you really want to know! But I don't see that you *need*. I mean, you could wear your hair in a prettier style and lots of people have to wear glasses, but they wear nice ones.'

Susan became more and more nervous. She backed towards the door with a scared expression.

'Er . . . good night, Fenella. Good night.'

Fenella replied shortly, and Susan shut the door with thankfulness. A moment later it was thrown open again and Fenella stood there frowning.

76

'If you repeat a word of this conversation to anyone, Susan Lambert . . .' she threatened fiercely.

'Oh, Fenella . . . I wouldn't . . . I won't!' Susan gasped, and fled. Oh, dear, she seemed to have a positive genius for getting into people's bad books. Now she supposed Fenella wouldn't be so friendly towards her.

Susan looked out of the landing window as she ran down the stairs. It had been raining all the afternoon, but now the rain had stopped. Between the finish of prep and their light supper of milk and biscuits the girls were allowed half an hour in the garden if weather permitted it. Susan suddenly decided that she would run down to the stables with the biscuit she had saved for Cobber from tea. Almost every day she managed a titbit for him, even if it was only a crust and he seemed to welcome it. She felt around in her pocket for her offering. It was somewhat crumbled now, but Cobber would probably appreciate it nevertheless.

Susan took a roundabout way across the garden. After the scene with Terry that afternoon it seemed more than usually necessary to keep her devotion to Cobber a secret. Beryl, however, spotted her almost at once.

'Oh, there you are, Susan. Going to the stables? Wait for me.'

Susan halted unwillingly. Though she racked her brains she could think of no way to dismiss Beryl. The other girl thrust her arm through Susan's, looking important.

'Terry's just furious with you,' she told her, giggling. 'You ought to have heard her just now, scolding Dumpling for sticking to old Meggie instead of bagging Cobber this term!'

'But I thought *Terry* wanted Cobber . . . !'

'She wants someone to share Cobber and Dallas as Rosemary did,' Beryl said shrewdly. 'She knows old Dumpling will do anything that's asked of her, so she could have Cobber then when she fancied him. I'm jolly glad I don't have to share my pony!'

Beryl ran to Whisky's loose box and patted his glossy head. 'You're all mine, aren't you, old boy?'

Feeling rather bleak, Susan fed Cobber with the remains of the biscuit and gained a little consolation from his obvious recognition of her.

'I'll give you some of Whisky's oats while Masters is out of the way, shall I?' chattered Beryl, making the best of her moment. 'Dad sent down a big bag from the farm and I know where it was put. Masters didn't seem half as pleased as I should have thought he would have been.'

'Well, didn't Masters say . . . ?' began Susan uncertainly.

'Oh, he's stuffy. Let's give them a treat. They'll love it.' Beryl dragged a large bag of oats forward, disregarding Susan's protest. She thrust in her hand, and Susan, after a moment's hesitation, followed suit.

'Don't give Cobber that!' Terry's voice came sharply from behind the two girls. Susan started guiltily, scattering some of the oats on the stable floor.

'Don't you realize we're trying to get the ponies in extra-good condition for the gymkhana?' stormed Terry. 'Masters knows exactly how much they need to eat. He doesn't like us to interfere with the feeding. You must know that!'

'I . . . I'm sorry,' faltered Susan. 'I . . . I didn't mean . . .'

'Didn't mean?' Terry pushed forward angrily, her hands clenched. 'You're so—so selfish you just do whatever pleases you for the moment! You didn't mean to lame Cobber either, I suppose! You'll be saying you *didn't mean* to adopt him as your special, when you knew all the time that I wanted him!'

'Why should you have him any more than me? You had Dallas.'

It was quite true, but Terry was in no mood to own it. She pushed forward obstinately, trying to get near Cobber, but Susan's back was pressed against the door of his box, preventing her. They were both breathing quickly, their faces red and angry.

'Get out of my way!'

Susan threw up her head defiantly.

'Why should I?'

Masters' quiet, drawling voice broke in from behind the two girls.

'I think both of you young leddies had better get back to school as fast as you can. The supper-bell went several minutes ago.' The old man's red-brown eyes held an amused gleam as they flicked swiftly over them, but his mouth was serious as he continued: 'Any more quarrelling over Cobber and I speak to

Miss Duncan about it. Maybe she'd say Meggie and Jimmy could be your mounts in the future.'

'Meggie and Jimmy?' Terry's eyes blazed indignantly, then fell before Masters' cool stare. 'All right, I'm sorry. You won't have any more trouble from me!' She marched out of the stables, her head held high.

Beryl stood waiting for Susan, her face expressing her satisfaction at having been a witness to the scene. Susan threw her a quick glance. She wanted to talk to Masters; to ask him if he thought she should give up Cobber for Terry, but with Beryl there it seemed difficult. She muttered, 'I'm sorry too, Masters,' and had to leave it at that.

As they went towards the school, Beryl was full of the quarrel, but Susan scarcely said a word. She felt shaken and upset. She had wanted so badly to be friendly with Terry and everything seemed bound to go wrong. Something that Beryl was saying about the coming Gymkhana arrested her attention.

'What was the date?' she interrupted Beryl to ask.

'The date of the Gymkhana? Why, the twenty-third. Why do you want to know that?' Beryl was looking at Susan curiously.

'Oh, nothing . . .' Susan said carelessly. Her mind was working swiftly. Somehow she must get Cobber in trim before that. He must jump again . . . he would jump again. The thing to do was to get him really used to her. Dad had always said that to get a horse in complete sympathy with one was half the battle.

'The Gymkhana will be fun, won't it?' Beryl was saying. 'It's a shame you haven't a pony of your own, isn't it? Of course, I shall be able to enter Whisky for all the events, while you——' she stopped. Even so selfish a person as Beryl was a little ashamed of herself for that remark.

Susan bit her lip. She had forgotten that. She hadn't realized that whatever she herself could do with Cobber, she would not be the only one to ride him. There would be other girls in other Forms who considered him their own property, too. Susan racked her brains for details of the Gymkhana arrangements as far as they had been given her, and one sentence came back with such sharp disappointment that it was almost a pain. 'No one is allowed to compete in more than two events.'

Susan felt quite hopeless. Only two! If she was best on Cobber, surely it wasn't fair that others should be allowed to ride him? Common sense, however, told her that it certainly would not be fair if others were not given their chance. She sighed. There had been a long pause and Beryl felt a little uncomfortable.

'You're not offended because I said that about Whisky, are you, Susan?' she asked anxiously.

'Why should I be?' Susan looked up, surprised. Her thoughts had been far away from Beryl, but she certainly wasn't going to take her into her confidence. 'You're lucky, that's all. You can't help it that this silly school has all kinds of ridiculous rules. I hate everything here,' she went on resentfully.

'I wish I hadn't come here. I wish I was back in Rhodesia.'

'Look . . .' Beryl swallowed hard and made a real effort to be generous. It might be policy, in any case, to keep in with Susan. 'I say, Susan, I . . . I might lend Whisky to you for one of the races. The bending race or . . . no, perhaps Musical Chairs might be better. Well, anyway, it would depend on how Whisky takes to you. He might not like anyone else riding him. . . .' The generous impulse was fast slipping away.

Susan's head went up proudly.

'Thank you very much, Beryl,' she said coldly. 'But you really needn't bother about me.'

If Susan had leaped eagerly at the offer, Beryl might have retreated further, but as it was she now insisted eagerly:

'No, honestly, Susan, I'd like to have you borrow Whisky for one of the events. I was just thinking out which race would be best for you, because of course you don't know Whisky like I do.'

Susan smiled suddenly.

'That's really very nice of you, Beryl. We'll see, shall we? You might change your mind again, and I really do know how you feel about it. I guess—I guess I might feel the same. Anyway, it's quite a long while ahead yet. We needn't decide now.'

'All right, then. We'll leave it for now,' Beryl agreed cheerfully. In spite of herself a feeling of relief swept over her. One never knew. Anything might happen before the Gymkhana. She hailed Pat as they entered the cloakroom and Susan was left alone.

Susan was standing at the foot of the stairs when Jacqueline called to her.

'If you're going upstairs now, Susan, would you just take this book along to Matron's room, please? I promised to let her have it this evening.'

Susan held out her hand for the book somewhat lethargically, and Jacqueline's blue eyes looked down at her with a considering expression.

'Are you approving of English life any more these days, Susan?'

There was a teasing note in the Head Girl's voice, and Susan looked up startled. How did Jacqueline know . . . ? What had someone been telling her . . . ?

'It's different . . .' she said awkwardly.

Jacqueline nodded.

'I imagine so. Well, Susan——' Her expression changed, and she went rather pale. Susan saw her hand go to the banister rail and tighten, the knuckles showing white.

'What is it? Aren't you well, Jacqueline?'

Jacqueline relaxed again and smiled.

'I've been having a bit of a pain, that's all. I say, don't say anything about it, Susan.' She hesitated, then went on briskly: 'Well, you'll take the book straight to Matron, won't you? Good night, Susan.'

Susan went on up the stairs feeling somewhat concerned. She hoped Jacqueline really was all right. She had looked dreadfully ill for a moment. Then her mind went back to Jacqueline's teasing remark about English life. She felt rather uncomfortable about it and, remembering various grumbles, wished she had not said so much. She entered her dormitory, later, in a humble mood. Terry's back was towards her. Susan touched her arm.

'Terry, I'm really sorry about Cobber. If I had known you felt like that about him I would have had Dallas instead.'

Terry shrugged her shoulders.

'Oh, well, it's over now. It doesn't matter.'

Susan stood there awkwardly for a moment, then went to her own cubicle. The apology had been difficult to make and Terry hadn't been very gracious about it. All the same she was glad she had made it. Her thoughts returned to Jacqueline. She did hope she was all right.

# 9

## Fenella Steps Up

MISS DUNCAN'S expression was graver than usual as she mounted the platform to take the morning prayers.

'I am very sorry to have to tell you, girls, that Jacqueline was taken ill during the night with acute appendicitis. She is in hospital now, and will be operated on this morning. We shall pray for the successful conclusion of her illness,' the Headmistress finished gravely.

A gasp of dismay went up from the assembled girls. It was quickly stifled as Miss Duncan raised her hand and bowed her head. Some of the little ones, slightly overwhelmed by the solemnity of the moment and the shock of hearing that their beloved Jacqueline was in trouble, found their eyes misting with tears and each bowed head hid a face which showed varying signs of sorrow and concern.

Both as a Head Girl and as a person, Jacqueline Graham was much admired. Fenella might be the sergeant-major of Westways School, but Jacqueline was its efficient and popular commanding officer. As the chief recreative interest of most of the girls was at the stables, it was natural that her splendid horsemanship and keenness for riding were considered almost necessary qualities of a Head Girl. Jacqueline commanded both respect and affection, for even she could be strict, though her sunny smile and sweet voice took the sting out of her reprimands in a way which was completely different from Fenella's brusque manner.

The prayer concluded, Miss Duncan's voice lifted again.

'We shall all be thinking of Jacqueline today, of course. The doctor assures me that everything possible will be done, and we shall hope to have good news of her soon. Meanwhile,' she paused and smiled down at the serious faces below her, 'we will all be as cheerful as possible and make plans for the future. It is unlikely that Jacqueline will be returning to school this term, so I have decided that Fenella Parsons shall be acting Head Girl for the remaining weeks. I hope you will all make things as easy as possible for her. I am sure it will please our invalid as well as myself if you will give Fenella the support and affection you have always given to Jacqueline.'

Had Miss Duncan chosen her words deliberately? the girls wondered as they filed soberly to their classrooms. Did she know the double shock she had given them in not only informing them of Jacqueline's illness, but also in announcing the name of her successor? Support might be just possible, but affection seemed almost a laughable word to apply to Fenella. Why, everyone said that she had a positive genius for making one feel rebellious, even if one knew that one was in the wrong.

'If I can love Fenella, then I'm more of a saint than I thought I was!' declared Terry dramatically, voicing the general opinion of the Fourth Form. She flopped into her desk in the classroom and fanned herself in mock exhaustion.

'Shades of the Army!' muttered Jennifer. 'She'll probably have us doing everything by numbers before we know where we are.'

Pat banged her books into her desk crossly.

'I do think Miss Duncan might have had a little feeling for us,' she grumbled. 'Admittedly we haven't anyone who could really take Jacqueline's place, but if Hazel or Lesley had been chosen as acting Head Girl, we might have had *some* fun.'

'We'll manage to have some fun all right! Just watch us. I refuse to be absolutely cowed by Fenella Parsons!' muttered Terry rebelliously.

Susan took a deep breath. She couldn't help it if she only made herself more unpopular. She owed it to Fenella to put in a word for her.

'Fenella isn't so bad when you get to know her, really,' she said earnestly.

The other girls looked at her curiously, and Terry gave a hoot of derision.

'My goodness!' she said slowly. 'Don't tell me you've fallen for Fenella's charms! Hold me up, someone!'

Jennifer giggled.

'You did say *charms*?' she inquired innocently, peering at Terry with mock sympathy. 'My poor child, you couldn't have had your eyes tested when you came to Westways. Most neglectful, most neglectful. I must see about it.'

Susan's face flushed, but her chin tilted defiantly and she stuck to her point.

'I meant what I said. Fenella has been awfully decent to me. I know she isn't . . . couldn't be quite like Jacqueline, but . . .' Her voice trailed away uncomfortably under the unsympathetic stares of the others, then, reviving, finished desperately. 'Well, I think, at any rate, we ought to give her a fair chance. . . .'

There was a long pause. Most of the girls looked at

87

Terry for guidance. Some of them thought it was rather cheek on Susan's part, considering she was only a new girl; but Terry was the acknowledged leader of the Form, and if she was willing to accept this way of looking at it, they would follow. But Terry made no move. She shrugged her shoulders as if to dismiss the subject, and it was Elizabeth, the charitable, who came to Susan's rescue.

'I agree with Susan. We ought to back Fenella up, if it's only for Jacqueline's sake. You heard what Miss Duncan said.'

Terry turned on her heatedly.

'Dumpling, you're too good to live, I know! What I didn't know was that Susan is, too. It's a bit of a shock to me.' She broke off as Jennifer muttered quickly:

'Look out, Terry! Here comes Miss Brooks!' and lowering her head as the History Mistress entered the room, whispered wickedly, 'Ah, this is where we become historical instead of hysterical!'

She put on her most innocent expression, but the other girls could not quite hide the giggles which convulsed them and were sternly suppressed by Miss Brooks.

To most of the girls at Westways that morning seemed particularly long. In the Fourth Form especially there was more than the usual amount of day-dreaming and inattention. Thoughts would keep straying to the hospital or to the dismal possibilities of Fenella's harsh reign. Perhaps the mistresses understood at least the first of these reasons and made allowances. At any rate Terry, at lunch-time, declared severely that it was a miracle that no one had achieved a bad mark.

'You speak for yourself, my dear!' Jennifer grinned across at her teasingly. 'You were certainly one of the worst offenders, and I must say I was both surprised and grieved to hear you inform Miss Brooks that Henry the Fourth had eight wives. Especially as you went to see the play in the holidays!'

Terry pouted, her eyes sparkling with mischief.

'It was a very understandable mistake, I consider. I thought she was talking about the other one—was it the eighth? Oh yes, that was the big fat one. I must say I think it's very silly of them to name so many of the kings alike. The Richards are bad enough, but the Henrys absolutely beat me!'

Beryl's face was long and tragic.

'How can you laugh and joke when poor darling Jacqueline is even now perhaps at death's door!' she reproved them dramatically.

Now that the Head Girl was ill she had suddenly discovered an almost sentimental affection for her which had certainly not been apparent before. Terry flushed deeply at the rebuke. Under her rebellion and her fun lurked a very genuine sense of sorrow and anxiety which had been nagging at her all the morning. It was just her way to try and throw it off, but now she felt ashamed of her flippancy and relapsed into silence.

Towards the end of the meal one or two girls

noticed that Miss Duncan had slipped out of the room. Now, as they stood up for grace, she hurried back. The expression on her face told them that all was well. She smiled at the girls reassuringly and announced cheerfully:

'I have some good news from the hospital, girls. Sister tells me that the operation has been quite successful and Jacqueline is comfortable. That is all we can expect at the moment, of course, but there is no reason to suppose that she will not gradually improve.'

Terry, who had been whispering quickly to the girls nearest to her, now lifted her hand, her face rather red.

'Yes, Terry?' Miss Duncan prompted encouragingly.

'Please, could we send Jacqueline our love and . . . speaking for the Fourth Form, we should like to give her something . . . fruit or flowers. . . .'

There was a subdued murmur of agreement from everyone, and Miss Duncan nodded.

'That's a nice idea, Terry. Certainly I'll send love from all of us, shall I? Later on, I'm sure Jacqueline will be very pleased to receive letters from all of you, and we might arrange for gifts of fruit and flowers to be sent to the hospital for her also. As you were the one to mention it, Terry, I suggest that you should represent the school from the Fourth Form downwards and collect contributions and suggestions. You, Lesley, might do the same for the Seniors. In that way we shall ensure that our gifts are suitably spaced over the time that Jacqueline has to be in hospital.'

Now that the tension was relieved Terry's spirits went up again with a bound. As they left the dining-hall, Fenella was standing by the door as usual, watching them go out. After passing her, Terry made a little grimace and muttered disgustedly:

'. . . Acting Head Girl . . . ! I'm sure Westways has never before had a Head Girl who can't even *ride* properly!'

'Ah,' said Jennifer. 'Maybe we shall see her down at the stables now. In her position she'll surely have to try and improve.' She giggled. 'I can see her covering herself with glory in the Gymkhana this year.'

'What, Fenella . . . ? When she never rides anything but poor old short-legged Jimmy! She looks just like a large sack of potatoes!'

Unknown to the speakers, Fenella had come up just behind them and caught the remark. Susan, having been compulsorily detained by Miss Woods' insistence on the tidy folding of her table-napkin, was near enough to see Fenella's face flush a deep red. She didn't look so much angry as miserable, Susan thought. Then Fenella turned, and seeing Susan just behind her, put on her sternest expression.

'No loitering in the corridors, Susan Lambert!' she snapped crossly. 'Hurry up, please. You should be in your classroom.'

'Yes, Fenella.' Susan accepted the rebuke meekly. Somehow she understood that the giving of it gave the older girl some relief from her feelings. It was a shame, really, that on her first day as Head Girl she should have heard the girls laughing at her riding. Susan wondered idly why Fenella had come to Westways if she didn't like riding. She just couldn't understand anyone not liking it. Would she dare to introduce the subject one evening? Susan dismissed the thought at once. She had already criticized Fenella's appearance. Surely that was bad enough? She did hope the girls weren't going to be really horrid, though.

As she moved towards her desk in the Fourth Form classroom, Susan noticed that Terry was drawing something on a piece of paper. She finished it with a flourish and passed it across to Jennifer, a wicked look in her eyes. Susan leaned forward, and now she could see that it was a cruelly lifelike caricature of Fenella awkwardly astride a small fat pony. Terry had drawn the pony's head turned towards its rider inquiringly, a haughty expression on his face. From the balloon which issued from its mouth came the words:

*'My dear girl, I'm not the greengrocer's pony!'*

Remembering Fenella's bleak expression in the corridor, Susan on a sudden impulse snatched the paper from Jennifer's hand as Miss Carr entered the room. She rammed it into her pocket quickly; but Terry, her temper rising, tried to get it back. Susan's hand closed firmly on her pocket, resisting, and then Miss Carr's voice came sharply from the desk.

'Susan Lambert, what are you doing? Go to your desk at once!'

Susan took her seat, her face flushed and her lips compressed. She tried hard to interest herself in the lesson, but she could sense the disapproval of the whole Form. Terry was popular and her clever caricatures had enlivened many a dull moment. Those who had not seen her latest effort would feel defrauded and indignant, she knew; but during the lesson Susan's hand went to her pocket more than once, and somehow she contrived to tear the paper into tiny pieces. As soon as the lesson was over she found Terry standing over her accusingly.

'Give me that paper at once, please, Susan. You had no right to snatch it from Jennifer like that!'

Half-apologetically Susan's hand went to her pocket and she took out the tiny pieces and gave them to Terry. The other girl's face was a study.

'You tore it up . . . !' Terry's eyes were fiercely accusing.

Susan bit her lip. Would she never stop offending Terry for one reason or another?

'—I . . . Miss Carr might have asked to see it . . .' she stammered.

For a moment Terry looked convinced by the excuse. Then she glared again.

'You didn't tear it up because of that! I think you've got the most awful cheek. You needn't think it will make any of us love Fenella more because you're always championing her!'

Susan looked bleak. She supposed everyone else,

except perhaps Elizabeth, would agree with Terry.

In that conjecture she was about right. Susan, with only the best of intentions this time, had by her action only emphasized the Form's disapproval and increased her own unpopularity.

## 10

## Persistence Pays

Down at the stables more than one effort was made to stop Susan's appropriation of Cobber for her own use. But in this matter Masters proved a useful ally. Perhaps he guessed that there was something behind it all when Cobber suddenly became so popular with various riders who, until then, had seemed quite satisfied with their own mounts. At any rate he made it a rule that the girls could make no further changes until the Gymkhana was over.

'It's in your own interests,' he told them gruffly. 'You'll get the best results with the pony that knows you best. Don't forget there are likely to be quite a number of entries for the open events this year. We don't want outsiders to run away with all the prizes, do we?'

So Susan was left in temporary possession of

94

Cobber, though she couldn't help knowing that there were many who were annoyed by the position; mostly because of their allegiance to Terry. In her own dormitory it was obvious that Elizabeth was the one who kept the peace, and her sunny temper did much to offset the chilly attitude of the other two. There was never any open quarrel but Susan felt herself the odd one of the quartette. She made very little effort to improve the relationship, contenting herself as well as she could with her riding-lessons and Beryl's rather erratic friendship.

The Gymkhana was now foremost in everyone's thoughts. Miss Duncan, yielding to the popular desire and the girls' promise that they would work even harder because of it, had made a further small concession regarding the hours in which they could ride. Each morning those desirous of using the free time between tea and prep for schooling the ponies could put their names to a list on the notice-board. No one knew the method by which Miss Duncan juggled with the entries, but it worked out fairly enough and gained the enthusiasts an extra half-hour or two each week.

Susan's name, of course, went down on the list every morning with unfailing regularity.

'I believe Cobber's getting over his fright at last!' she told Beryl enthusiastically. 'At first I thought he'd never jump again, but yesterday he managed the sacks twice.'

'Pooh! The sacks are nothing! I want Whisky to clear the wall. He ought to be able to do it. Daddy said they told him that he had cleared four feet, but I think they were telling lies.' Beryl's face wore a disgusted look. 'Perhaps Daddy was really had over him. Do you think it would be a good idea to write and ask him for another pony instead?'

Susan looked horrified.

'Oh, Beryl, you wouldn't give Whisky up now, surely! Besides, Masters says he is really a fine little chap, and he'll be jolly good if you persevere.'

'I hate Masters. He's so horrid to me now.'

Susan looked a little awkward. She knew that Beryl had been so often rude and obstinate that the old man had lost patience with her.

'I only helps those as helps themselves and really wants to be helped,' he had muttered under his breath once when Beryl had tossed her head at some well-meant advice.

It was only just lately that Beryl, feeling worried that she was not getting the best out of her pony, had begun to defer to Masters again. But the old man had an obstinate streak, and now he either pretended not to hear when she appealed to him, or pretended that he was fully occupied elsewhere. To Susan he was unfailingly kind and encouraging, but when she implored him to tell her how soon he thought Cobber would get back his nerve and jump as he had done before, he shook his grey head.

'I can't say, Miss Susan. It might be tomorrow, and it might not be at all.'

'Not at all?' Susan looked aghast. 'Oh, but, Masters, I do want to jump in the Gymkhana!'

'Well, the others have given him up, miss, and are taking it in turns to jump the other ponies. Still, if you're very patient you might succeed even now. You can never tell with hosses. That little fellow had a big scare, don't forget.'

Susan hung her head.

'I know, and it was my fault. I feel awful every time I think about it. But I'm going on trying. Even apart from the Gymkhana itself, I feel that I owe it to Cobber to get him back to what he was. I know that he really loved jumping before, and I spoiled it for him. Masters, I'm sure if I'm really patient with him he'll get over it.' There was appeal in Susan's eyes, but Masters shook his head again.

'As I said afore, miss, there's no telling.' Then a twinkle came into the old groom's eyes. 'But there, I always says that when a woman really sets her mind on a thing she's awful like to get it.'

'You think so?' Susan's face was alight with hope. 'Oh, Masters, then I ought to win, because my mind is *very* set on curing him!'

Thinking of this conversation now, Susan searched the notice-board hopefully for her name. Joyfully she saw that it was down for that very day. The previous afternoon had been that allotted to the Fourth Form's riding lesson. She reminded herself that Cobber, for the first time, had consented to jump the sacks, and that in spite of two or three subsequent refusals he had repeated the performance just before their time was up. If she could persuade him to do as well today she would really begin to feel that he was on the up-grade.

As soon as tea was over, Susan dashed upstairs to change. Each minute was precious, and in spite of the fact that, as always, that fact seemed to make one slower than ever, she was ready in a surprisingly short time. Susan ran down the garden and past the orchard towards the stables. The sun was shining brightly. The apple trees were a mass of pink-and-white blossom, and the birds were singing so loudly that it seemed as if they would burst their small throats.

Susan had to admit to herself, if grudgingly, that early summer in England was a beautiful time. For the first time for days her mind went back to Rhodesia. That, too, was beautiful beyond believing sometimes. Susan remembered the long avenues as she had seen them when visiting Salisbury. Long lanes of a heavenly mauve colour and woods just like fairyland with their carpets of mauve flowers; flowers something like the Canterbury bells that grew in England. They used to put them on the ends of their fingers, making them long and thin like the hands of an old witch.

But it was the smell of the gardens which was so beautiful in England. People used to say that Rhodesia was famous for its rivers which have no water, its flowers which have no smell and its birds which have no song. Actually it wasn't quite true, because some of the flowers did smell, only then it was quite overpowering like the smell of the frangipanni and the orange blossom that made one feel sick with its sweetness. But here the apple trees had a lovely smell which made Susan sniff appreciatively and the birds were singing sweetly. As for rivers, Susan laughed to herself, if there was one thing one had too much of in England, it was water!

Susan shook herself suddenly, realizing how her feet had slowed down with her thoughts. The precious half-hour must not be wasted.

When she arrived at Cobber's box, Susan patted Cobber's head and spoke to him. She always fancied he gave his acknowledgment of her greeting when he pushed his soft nose into her hand.

'No biscuits today, darling,' she told him regretfully. 'It's so dreadfully hard to keep them for you, and you did have one yesterday.' She threw his bridle over his head, tightening the buckles expertly. As she saddled him she turned and saw the stable boy, Tom, watching her with a curious expression on his face. He lowered his eyes when she looked up, and she said, on a sudden impulse:

'Did your friend find his sheep that day?'

The boy stared at her blankly.

'Friend . . . ? What friend, miss?'

'Oh, you know.' Susan regretted her remark. She was anxious to get on with her riding and the question had been an idle one. She threw the words over her shoulder impatiently. 'You were talking to your friend that day up in the high field—a man in tweeds.'

Tom's light eyes stared back at her with a half-frightened expression.

'Don't know what you're talking about, miss,' he said flatly.

Susan shrugged her shoulders. It was rather funny but she certainly had no time to waste and it was really nothing to do with her. She swung her leg over the saddle and rode Cobber into the field. Masters was hailing her with a friendly wave.

'At it again?' The old man grinned as he detained her to tighten a girth strap.

'Yes, I'm hoping Cobber will do even better than he did yesterday.' Susan bent down to him confidently. 'I did tell you that he jumped the sacks twice yesterday?'

'You did, miss; more than once.' Masters' eyes twinkled.

'Well, if he does them again today, could I try him over the brush?'

The old man stroked his chin.

'Why, yes, I think you might. I shall be within call if you want me.'

'All right.' Susan suddenly realized that none of the other girls had come down to the field. She seemed to be the only one riding that afternoon. Remarking the fact to Masters, he nodded.

'Miss Duncan mentioned there were various reasons for it, miss. Music lessons and that end-of-term concert Miss Lesley is getting up.'

'Oh yes, that. Thank heaven I'm not musical.'

Masters was waving a hand towards the gate.

'It seems you won't be the only one after all, Miss Susan,' he said tersely. Susan fancied the look on his weather-beaten face was almost contemptuous. She turned her head as he strode away and saw Fenella coming through the gate.

Fenella! Then Terry's carelessly spoken words were coming true after all. She was wearing her jodhs, so she must be going to ride. It was certainly unusual. In spite of the fact that she was wasting more of her precious time, Susan waited. It seemed rude not to do so—besides, she was a little curious. Fenella looked embarrassed as she lifted a hand in greeting to the younger girl.

'Hallo, Susan. I didn't think anyone else was riding this afternoon.' It seemed to Susan that Fenella's voice was dispirited.

'Are you . . . are you going to school one of the ponies?' she asked a little timidly.

Fenella smiled wryly.

'I shouldn't think of dignifying my performance with that expression, Susan. I'm just going to try and stop on. I still think Jimmy is about the easiest for that, don't you?'

'Oh, not Jimmy!' The words came from Susan impulsively.

'Why not?' Fenella stood arrested. 'I'm no good at riding, you know, only I thought I ought to make a bit of a show.'

'Well . . . er . . . Jimmy is so short and fat and your legs are so long. Couldn't you . . . couldn't you ride . . . well, say, Muffet, for instance?'

Fenella coloured.

'My dear child, I'm not Jacqueline. I'm only trying to take her place.'

'Oh, well . . . I just thought . . .' Susan rode Cobber away before Fenella could say anything else. Who was *she* to advise a Prefect, anyway?

Fenella gazed after Susan thoughtfully. Had she been making fun of her? Everyone knew, of course, that she couldn't ride for toffee, and it was only the feeling that, now she was Head Girl, she should make an effort that had prompted her to ride that afternoon. She had not expected to meet anyone down at the field, and she had formed the vague idea of asking Masters for a little tuition. Now she went to the door of Muffet's box and regarded her speculatively. The mare looked enormously tall after Jimmy, but perhaps Susan was right and she did look top-heavy on the small pony. Fenella remembered that Terry had said that she looked like a sack of potatoes on a horse.

With sudden determination Fenella moved forward. Muffet shied restlessly, and she drew back, a little scared. She caught sight of Masters and called to him as he crossed the yard. He came across to her, and she asked him impulsively:

'Masters, *could* I ride Muffet, do you think?'

Masters stroked his chin reflectively. There had been a note of pleading in Fenella's voice. Perhaps he had been mistaken and this brusque-mannered girl was not so dull and lumpy as she appeared. Many a time he had indulged in a quiet laugh to himself at the ludicrous picture she made on Jimmy. She might be worth helping. Well, he would try it once. No more.

'Why, yes, Miss Fenella,' he broke the silence gravely, 'I should certainly have a change. You are too big for Jimmy, that's flat. Don't be nervous of Muffet. She's well-mannered as a rule; but horses can sense your attitude, you know, and nerves affect them so that it brings out all the worst of them.'

Fenella was listening with such attention that Masters took a sudden liking to her. He continued: 'I was watching you just now, Miss Fenella, and your approach was wrong. You startled Muffet, and of course she shied. You should speak to her first, pat her back and make her feel at ease. Then when you saddle and bridle her she knows what you're at and takes no offence.'

'I see,' Fenella said, with a new meekness. 'Er . . . thank you, Masters.'

Together they saddled Muffet, and a few minutes later Fenella, looking flushed and determined, rode across the yard.

'All right?' Masters looked up at the girl with a twinkle in his eyes. 'You certainly look much better on that horse, young lady. A fine figure of a girl like you can't look at her best on a small pony.'

'Thank you, Masters. Yes, I'll be quite all right now,' Fenella said gravely. Not for the world would she show him how nervous she was feeling. She hoped Muffet didn't know either or, according to Master's theory, anything might happen.

Out in the field Susan had elatedly taken Cobber across the filled sacks with no refusals at all. Now she urged him towards the brush with hope high in her heart.

'Good old boy. Ups-a-daisy!' she whispered softly.

Cobber strode forward. For a moment Susan thought he would do it. Then he stopped abruptly; so abruptly indeed that Susan slid from the saddle and banged her knee on the ground.

'Oh, Cobber, you *are* naughty,' she scolded him, rubbing her knee and making a wry face. A moment later she belied her words by kissing his nose and telling him that, even if he was, it was her fault and she didn't really blame him. Then she set her mouth in a determined line and mounted the pony again. 'All the same, young man, you're *not* going to get away with it. I shall keep on trying, so there!'

Twice more he refused, and Susan's heart sank very low. 'One more try,' she told him, 'then I'll have to go in because time is up. Now . . . ! Oh, Cobber darling, *do*!'

Whether the pleading in Susan's voice really transmitted itself through the soft brown ears she didn't know, but this time Cobber rose like a bird. She was up . . . and she was over, with a perfect landing!

'Oh, Cobber, beautiful darling Cobber, you're the nicest, cleverest pony in all the world!' Susan hugged his neck and, dismounting, gave him the two pieces of sugar she had been saving for such an occasion. Then she turned her head and saw Fenella riding sedately round the field. Spurring Cobber forward, she raced across and hailed her excitedly :

'Did you see? Did you see? Cobber jumped the brush—at last! I knew he would one day.'

Fenella nodded and smiled, but with a slightly withdrawn expression, Susan felt. Then she noticed the older girl's mount. Why, she had taken Muffet after all! Fenella looked ever so much better on the larger horse, really she did. In fact, if only she wouldn't hold her hands high and hunch her shoulders as if she was scared that at any moment she would take a header, she would look quite nice. For a moment Susan wondered daringly if she could possibly comment on these faults. But no, there were definite limits to which a Fourth Former could go with the Acting Head Girl of Westways School. It might even be as well if she didn't remark on the fact that Fenella had taken her advice regarding Muffet.

'I must go and tell Masters the good news!' she said suddenly and, wheeling, galloped off towards the stables. Masters might help her about Fenella. Susan had always got on well with the old man, and she knew that he would keep her secret if she took him into her confidence.

She would make Fenella popular yet!

## 11

## Visit to Jacqueline

THE hospital where Jacqueline was convalescing after her operation was only about a mile from Westways School. As soon as the girls heard that the invalid was well enough to receive visitors there was great competition for the honour.

Once more Miss Duncan's ingenuity was tested in order to devise a fair scheme by which each girl who so desired it should have an equal chance to be among the favoured few. Each day two visitors were allowed to the hospital and every morning at prayers the names of the fortunate ones were drawn from a hat containing named slips of paper representing almost every member of the school. It was a point of honour to include oneself in the draw but Susan's feelings at having her name drawn one morning were rather mixed. She was pleased to be chosen for the honour, of course, and she liked Jacqueline very much, but her pleasure was tempered with shyness, especially when her companion on the expedition proved to be Lesley Grainger. The shy, dreamy Prefect, with her single-minded passion for music, was not really awe-inspiring, but Susan was uncomfortably conscious of the difference in their age and position, and would much rather have gone with one of her own Form. She imagined herself sitting mum beside Jacqueline's bed while her two elders did the talking, and would have got out of the whole thing if only she had known how.

Setting off after school that afternoon with Lesley, Susan felt tongue-tied and strange. As she walked along the road beside the older girl she was thinking of Cobber. It would be Monday now before she could try him over the brush again. She hoped fervently that he would not have forgotten how to do it by that time.

So deep was she in her thoughts that Susan scarcely noticed that Lesley was silent too. As they reached the hospital gates she glanced up at her companion and wondered rather guiltily if she had thought her rude. But Lesley, obviously, was far away in a world of her own. It was a world of music, not of riding, Susan guessed, for every now and then a little sound emerged from Lesley's lips, a soft snatch of a tune which Susan only vaguely recognized. She realized suddenly that, left alone, Lesley would have wandered on past the gates of the hospital, and steered her through them with an amused giggle. Lesley came back to her surroundings with a start, and looked guilty.

'Gracious!' she remarked. 'I hadn't realized that we had arrived. Sorry, Susan.' Speaking briskly to cover her embarrassment at being thus found wanting by a mere Fourth-Former, she went on: 'It's this way, Susan. I've been before, of course.'

She took over the lead and with a return of her shyness Susan followed her down a long white-walled passage. The floor was covered with green rubber and there was a strong smell of disinfectant. Susan wrinkled her nose disgustedly. She had not been in a hospital before and she decided now that she didn't particularly want to come again.

They turned a corner and, after a brief knock, entered a room all cream-and-white paint, where Jacqueline was propped up in bed and smiling at them. The room was full of flowers and Jacqueline herself looked happy and comfortable and very pretty in a pale pink dressing jacket. Maybe hospitals were rather nice after all, thought Susan. At any rate the Head Girl seemed to be a very good advertisement for them. Jacqueline greeted her visitors enthusiastically but Susan only smiled shyly and took a chair on the farther side of the bed, leaving the others to make conversation. Once or twice they tried to draw her into their talk but presently they gave it up and only chatted to each other.

A very pretty nurse, with fluffy hair, came in presently with Jacqueline's tea on a dainty tray. She seemed full of fun and teased her patient in a friendly sort of way. A few minutes after she had left them she put her head round the door of the room again and spoke to Lesley, with an apologetic smile.

'It's a shame to disturb you, dear, but would you just have a word with Madame Melanie? I happened to mention that you were here and told her you hadn't come to see her this time, but she insists on seeing you. Poor old dear, she's rather fractious today. It would be doing her a favour.'

'Of course I'll come.' Lesley jumped up at once. 'You don't mind, Jacqueline? I shan't stay long.'

'You go, of course,' smiled Jacqueline. 'And give her my love.' She turned to Susan as Lesley hurried away. 'Poor old lady. She's been in here for some months now. She used to teach music at Westways, you know, and she has never forgotten Lesley, though she was only in one of the lower Forms at the time. Madame Melanie always predicts that Lesley will be a famous violinist some day. She will too, you know,' she finished seriously. 'Lesley's really good.'

Susan nodded, not knowing much about it, but recognizing something quite out of the ordinary both in Lesley's ability and her personality. She was startled, the next moment, by the change on Jacqueline's face as she bent towards Susan and said quickly: 'Now that she's gone I can talk to you, Susan. I wanted to see you alone really. You see . . .' She hesitated, then went on quickly: 'I can trust you not to repeat this conversation, can't I? Lesley's so dreamy and Hazel's wrapped up in sports. I can't gather much from them. Susan . . . how is Fenella getting on with the girls?'

Susan's mouth opened in surprise.

Jacqueline nodded understandingly.

'Oh, I guess it seems queer that I should ask you that, but since you are the one who works with Fenella you must have got to know her better than the others. Do you like her?'

Susan's face reddened slowly.

'I do like her, Jacqueline, but the others . . .' She hesitated and looked awkward.

'The others don't. That's right, isn't it?'

'Well, you know how Fenella . . .' Susan felt for the right word. It seemed all wrong to use the phrase 'bosses everyone' to Jacqueline, but it was the only one which would come into her mind.

Jacqueline nodded again and looked worried. Then she gave a little grin which made her look very young.

'Fenella's rather like a hedgehog, you know. She's prickly outside but inside she's really a nice creature. I've been a little afraid that the girls have never found out the inside part of Fenella.'

'I have——' Susan said shyly.

'Look, Susan, will you do something for me?'

'Oh, anything.' Susan's tone was fervent. Apart from being really fond of Jacqueline, as everyone was, it made her very proud to be taken into the Head Girl's confidence.

'Well, keep on working quietly for Fenella behind the scenes, will you? It might help a little. I expect it will be rather hard as you're still quite a new girl. I wouldn't ask you, only I happen to know that already you've helped quite a bit.'

'I have . . . ?' Susan's mouth opened again and her eyes nearly popped out of her head.

Jacqueline smiled sagely.

'Little birds tell me things, you know. I'm also rather good at putting two and two together and making four; even four-and-a-half sometimes, perhaps. I know, for instance,' Jacqueline's voice lowered solemnly, 'that Fenella has ordered some new glasses —nice ones with flesh-coloured rims. And she's riding Muffet. . . .'

At that moment footsteps were heard hurrying along the corridor and Jacqueline just had time to add under her breath, 'Keep it up, Susan,' when Lesley entered, breathless and apologetic.

'I'm so sorry to have been so long, Jacqueline. Poor old Madame was so pleased to see me and I just couldn't get away from her before. I do hope Susan has been entertaining you properly.'

Jacqueline poured out another cup of tea and handed it across to Lesley.

'Oh yes, I've been hearing a lot about school. By the way, I'm so glad to know that Cobber is gradually recovering from his fright,' she said demurely.

Susan almost choked on her tea and had to turn away to hide her confusion. So Jacqueline knew that too. There didn't seem much that she did not know.

As she and Lesley left the hospital and walked back to school through a misty rain, Susan pondered over the conversation. The little feeling of pride because of Jacqueline's confidence remained with her, but now it was somewhat overcast by the realization of the difficulties that lay ahead. She really did like Fenella and wanted the other girls to like her too, but as for working for her as Jacqueline had suggested, well, she had tried it already once or twice and it hadn't improved her own position. It was all very nice and flattering to be on good terms with the Seniors but, when it came down to it, friends of one's own age was what one wanted most. She rather wished now that she had told Jacqueline that she was not very popular herself. That might have convinced her that there wasn't very much she could do about Fenella. Out of all the Fourth Form she hadn't a real friend, reflected Susan bleakly; unless one could count Beryl and she was as unpredictable and changeable as the English weather which, after a morning of brilliant sunshine, had degenerated into this miserable drizzle of rain. Susan had the uncomfortable feeling that Beryl would quickly transfer her allegiance to anyone who made a bid for it, and that their friendship was just a case of two rather unpopular birds flocking together.

She sighed heavily and Lesley, noticing her dismal expression as they turned into the school gates, remarked:

'It has turned out wretchedly, hasn't it? I guess we're both ready for a really decent tea. You couldn't call what we had at the hospital much, so I hope they've left us something.'

It somehow comforted Susan a little to be able to attribute her depression to the weather and she was grateful to Lesley for the suggestion. It was nice, too, to know that Lesley was human enough to like her comforts as much as most people, even if she was going to be a famous musician. Susan pushed her problems to the back of her mind and quite enjoyed the tea which Matron had kept for the late-comers in her room.

As Susan closed the door of Matron's room a little later Beryl came running along the corridor. She stopped when she saw Susan.

'Oh, hallo, you're back? I say, Terry played such a joke on Fenella this afternoon!' she gloated. 'I wish you could have seen her face!'

'What happened?' Susan asked rather faintly. Was this the sort of occasion when she should try and work on Fenella's behalf?

'Terry managed to get hold of Fenella's blazer, I don't know how. She sewed two paper crowns, one to each sleeve—representing a sergeant-major, of course. Fenella had the blazer over her arm as she was telling some of us off for playing about and suddenly she put it on and saw the crowns. It was too funny, because she had just been barking at us in that Army manner of hers.'

'What happened then?'

'Well, someone must have told Fenella that we call her our Sergeant-Major, because she seemed to jump to it at once. She tore the crowns off her sleeves and said very coldly: "The way some of you kids behave it seems you need a little Army discipline!" ' Beryl mimicked Fenella's manner with a giggle. 'And then she just walked away. I must say I was rather surprised that she didn't ask who had done it. So was Terry.'

Susan looked thoughtful as she went downstairs. She wished it hadn't been Terry who had played that trick. Fenella really seemed to have been quite decent about it, and it must have been rather horrid for her.

If only Terry, who was a sport, would recognize that Fenella was really trying!

Susan sighed. There didn't seem much she could do about it, this time.


## 12

## A Ride to Disaster

The girls gazed at Masters, quite dismayed.

'But we've such a lot of schooling to do if we're going to be ready for the Gymkhana! It wastes time just to go for a ride!' Terry's voice rose in an indignant wail.

Master's reply came in the voice which brooked no argument.

'Them's Miss Duncan's orders, Miss Terry. She doesn't want you to get stale; says a ride over the moors will do you good on a day like this.'

Terry pouted crossly. Dallas was beside her, all ready for mounting, and she threw her leg over the saddle with an indignant flourish. She reined the pony next to Nigger who had Jennifer up.

'I'd made up my mind to get Dallas over the wall today,' she grumbled. 'He can do it easily, I know, but he's been getting careless lately and always knocks two blocks off the top. I don't see why we should have to go for a ride if we don't want to.'

Susan, following just behind on Cobber, echoed Terry's sentiments. It was a bitter disappointment to her not to be able to jump Cobber, for he was still not quite certain of himself and there was so little time left. Beryl, on the other hand, had been so humiliated by her failure to make Whisky jump with any outstanding success that she welcomed a change. Her pony certainly looked a handsome little chap now as he responded to Beryl's urging and cantered past the other ponies into the lead.

Masters, however, riding Miss Duncan's Firebrand, sternly motioned her back into line, taking the lead himself. He was looking rather put out for, at the last moment, Tom had been prevented from joining them by a violent bilious attack and he usually relied on him to keep stragglers in line.

They cantered across the high field and through the white gate on to the moor, Susan's spirits rose as the ponies' hooves beat in soft rhythm on the springy purple heather and the keen sweet air entered her lungs. In the interests of schooling Cobber she had almost forgotten the exhilaration of a real ride and now rather welcomed Miss Duncan's ruling.

She thought that the ponies must be enjoying it, too, and found herself remembering other rides; wild gallops across country wilder and bleaker than this on the little Basuto ponies her father had kept. But already the image had faded a little and she found, surprisingly, that the ache of longing only came when she thought of her mother and father.

Susan wondered a little bleakly what it would be like spending the whole long summer holidays with Aunt Jane. She was very nice, of course, and had been awfully kind about sending letters and parcels since she had been at school. Still, it couldn't help but be dull and Susan thought enviously of Beryl and Terry and the others who were really going home. She threw off the thought impatiently and determined to make the most of the pleasure of the moment.

Before long it was evident that Susan was not the only one of the party who thought it pleasant to go for a ride again.

'Couldn't we go as far as Mandy's Tor, please, Masters?' begged Terry, her cheeks aglow with the exercise.

The old man drew his great round watch from his pocket and studied it with his usual deliberation.

'Yes, I think we could make it if we lose no time. No one is having any difficulties?'

There was a chorus of protest at the very idea and the little cavalcade rode on over the moor. They passed a tiny wandering brook that ambled over big stones to hurry down a deep drop in a miniature bubbling waterfall. Overhead the sun blazed down from a clear blue sky, drenching the heather with warmth, picking up diamonds from the sparkling water and casting long shadows from the green-clad trees. Susan felt completely in tune with Cobber as he moved easily under her. Forgetting the usual barrier she called gaily to Terry, 'Isn't this grand!' but Terry did not hear. Taking her silence for a snub Susan thought crossly: All right! If you don't want to be friendly I don't care. She rode swiftly to the head of the line to join Masters, unconsciously setting a faster pace for the whole party, for Firebrand was in good trim and the old man was enjoying himself.

Terry, lost in thoughts of her own, noticed nothing of this. She had, without realizing it, fallen well to the rear and presently Beryl's agitated manœuvres beside her forced themselves on her attention. Whisky seemed to be behaving badly. Beryl was holding the curb so tightly that the pony's mouth hung open and he moved restlessly from side to side.

'What's the matter?' asked Terry, reining Dallas in and watching them curiously.

'This . . . this beastly pony!' Beryl ground out the words through her teeth. 'He just won't do anything I tell him to this afternoon. He's bad-mannered and bad-tempered and I wish I'd never seen him.'

She pulled one-sidedly on the curb again. Whisky, his mouth paining him, veered sideways, shying violently. Terry, taken unawares, failed to pull Dallas clear and he kicked out a startled hoof. For Whisky it was the last straw.

Flustered by Beryl's harsh treatment and Dallas' close proximity he lurched and, catching the sharp edge of a stone on his foot to madden him further, turned with a snort and galloped away across the

117

heather for all he was worth. Beryl gave a shriek and, sitting very far forward, clung shamelessly to the crutch.

Terry called to the others but they were now well ahead and had not noticed the trouble. Soon they would be out of sight behind a narrow belt of trees which straggled across the moor. Terry had a moment of indecision. Beryl did not know the moor as well as she did. She was riding now in the direction of Devil's Bog and by the time Terry had gained the attention of the rest of the party Beryl would have secured a big start.

Terry wheeled Dallas round and galloped after Whisky. He was already well ahead and Beryl seemed to have lost all control and was now merely holding on grimly. Terry spurred Dallas forward, shouting:

'Pick up the reins, Beryl! Pull him in!'

But Beryl was past obeying instructions. Though she still clung on desperately she had lost all hope and was only waiting for the crash. Terry flicked Dallas with her crop and he responded at a smart pace. Whisky swerved again and disappeared behind a high pile of boulders. There was a faint scream and Terry heard Beryl calling her name. Oh heavens, surely it was not the bog already!

When Terry rounded the stone pyre there was no one to be seen. The ground dropped steeply here and a narrow path, thickly overgrown with bushes, disappeared downwards. Terry could feel the earth giving under the pony's feet as she urged Dallas forward. But he stopped dead with a little whinny, his ears pricked back.

Terry dug his sides sharply with her feet and tried to drive him, but Dallas would not budge. He only turned his head and gave Terry a reproachful look out of the corners of his eyes, showing the whites.

Terry made a sound of impatience and, dismounting, tied Dallas to a tree and ran down the steep, slippery slope ahead. Her feet slithered and one of them began to sink. She drew it back, with a startled gasp. She tried again in another place, but again her foot sank in a strangely cloying substance which drew her downwards.

She stepped backwards and found a foothold on the solid rock. Holding on to a sturdy shrub she bent forward at a precarious angle. Now she could just see Beryl. Whisky was sunk deep in the oozy substance. His head was held back awkwardly by Beryl's straining arms and his eyes were rolling.

'Oh . . . oh, Terry . . . !'

Beryl's voice had panic in it and Terry found herself infected. She glanced desperately behind her. Oh, why had she attempted to follow alone? At the time it had seemed better not to wait for Masters' help, but now she was powerless.

'Hold on, Beryl! I'll get help. Just hold on!'

Turning back, Terry untied Dallas and, throwing her legs across the saddle, rode swiftly back across the moor, despair in her heart. She knew these treacherous bogs of Dartmoor well. If Whisky . . . if Beryl . . . It did not bear thinking about.

Past the rock pile again she saw the riders silhouetted on the skyline. They were galloping towards her, Firebrand well ahead. Thank heaven they must have discovered quite soon that two of their party were missing. Now Terry could see Masters shading his eyes with his hand.

'Coo . . . eee! Coo . . . eee!' Terry forced Dallas across tufts of heather, waving and calling frantically. Masters drew close, his face grim and set.

'Quick! Beryl is caught in the bog. Over here!' Terry led the way and Masters, with a terse command to the girls to keep together and beware of the bog, followed closely. He tied Firebrand up beside Dallas and Terry showed him the path. Most of the girls decided to dismount also and they crowded together in the background, their faces concerned and anxious. Hearing Terry's explanation Susan was reminded of the remark that Jacqueline had made earlier in the term. How true her words had been! Dallas, the moorland pony, had recognized the danger, but Whisky, for all his breeding, had not.

Masters was scrambling down the slippery slope now, choosing the flat rocks for stepping stones and holding on to whatever scrub grew handy.

'Hold on, Miss Beryl!' he called. 'I'm coming. Don't let go. Someone bring me a bridle from one of the horses as quickly as pssible,' he directed over his shoulder tersely to the girls. 'It's all right, Miss Beryl. Don't panic.'

A moment later Susan and Terry ran forward together with a bridle each. They slithered down beside Masters, holding on to the scrub and trying to keep their feet firm.

'That's good. I'll probably need them both. Fool that I am not to carry a rope,' Masters muttered, shooting out a long arm.

'Now, Miss Beryl, catch on to this.'

'Oh . . . oh, I can't. I've missed it.'

'Pull yourself together!' Master ordered sternly. 'Try again! Now . . . !'

Beryl clutched wildly at the flying bridle and this time she caught it.

'Can you tie it?' shouted Masters. 'Or, better still, get it right over his head. Whoa, Whisky, steady, old fellow! We'll get you out in just a jiffy. Now, Miss Beryl, here comes another bridle. Tie them all together to give the greatest length. You can't? Well, unbuckle a strap and fit one in from the other bridle. Good girl. Now fling it back to me.'

Given something definite to do Beryl had managed to steady the trembling of her fingers sufficiently to fit the three bridles one into another so that they made a fair length. The girls watched breathlessly while she flung the leathers forward. Once, twice, Beryl missed and gave a hopeless little gesture as the improvised lifeline dangled in the muddy ooze below her. Her face looked white and strained.

'Once more,' Masters encouraged her. 'Now, try again. . . . Good girl. Now, all of you hang on behind me now with all the strength you can muster! Are you ready? Go!'

Masters stepped gradually backwards, the straps

wound tightly around his hands. Susan and Terry hung on behind him and pulled with all their might, others following suit, so that they made a strong chain.

Whisky, however, was very frightened and, refusing to move an inch, did nothing to help them. Beryl lost her nerve completely on finding that they were making no progress and, bursting into tears, hung limply across the pony's back. Masters did all he could to encourage her.

'Come along, Miss Beryl. You can't stay there all night,' he said at last. 'Not unless you want us to go off and leave you. We want our tea.'

'I . . . I don't know what . . . to do.' Beryl's voice came to the others plaintively.

'Do? Why, rouse up that pony of yours and *make* him move!'

Beryl picked up the reins again and with suddenly renewed hope kicked Whisky's sides and flicked him with her crop. For a few minutes he floundered bewilderedly in the dark ooze, not realizing what was wanted of him. Then with a great effort he dragged his feet forward and slowly and painfully moved towards Masters. Now the girls were pulling with all their strength behind the old man and with a squelching sound of hooves in the soft mud Whisky found himself on firmer ground at last. He jerked his head and shook himself to and fro, the black mud from his sides spraying out in a shower over all of them.

'Good old boy. Good chap. You've done it,' Masters

patted and soothed the exhausted pony. The tears were now running down Beryl's cheeks in a fresh spate.

'Oh, it was awful! It was so awful!'

Masters half lifted her off the saddle and on to one of the other ponies. The two bridles which had been used in the rescue were caked with dirt, and although they were wiped down as well as possible, Cobber and Dallas tossed their heads uneasily when they were put on.

'There's no help for it,' Masters said worriedly. 'They'll have to bear it, but you'll need to ride them as gently as you can. Whisky is not fit to be ridden at all. He's shivering now, and we'll be lucky if we don't have trouble with him.' Masters looked round the group swiftly. 'Miss Pat, you'll have to come up on Firebrand with me. I should think you're the lightest. Miss Susan, you can lead Whisky, and Miss Terry, you stay near Miss Beryl and keep an eye on her.'

Having got his little company into the best order he could, Masters led the way back across the moor. He looked grim and worried, and Susan guessed he was blaming himself for getting ahead and not noticing the trouble with Whisky.

And he probably wouldn't have done it if it hadn't been for me talking to him, Susan thought contritely. Beryl was still whimpering quietly, very sorry for herself.

'It was all Whisky's fault,' she wailed, to anyone who would listen. 'He's—he's a beastly pony and I hate him!'

## 13

## Vigil in the Night

IN spite of some feeling of sympathy for her in her fright, it was the general opinion that Beryl had made rather a mess of things.

'It could never have happened if she had been a good rider,' asserted Terry, as she got ready for bed that night.

'And that she never has been,' Jennifer said, a little bitterly. 'In spite of her immaculate togs and her "blood pony".'

'Poor Tiny, the immaculate togs hit you specially hard, don't they?' Elizabeth's round face grinned wickedly. 'By the way, what *did* your mother say on the subject of new jodhs?'

'She said,' Jennifer struck a dramatic attitude and frowned darkly, 'that it's not her fault that I shoot upwards like Jack's beanstalk; that I've already had two new pairs since the winter term and she just can't manage any more. I'll have to look a fool at the Gymkhana after all.'

'Oh, dearie, you didn't think new jodhs were going to prevent that?' Terry asked, with an innocent face.

Tiny advanced threateningly with a wet flannel.

'Wretch! Here——!'

'Now, children!' admonished Elizabeth, peaceably placing her plump person between the two scuffling girls. Susan, who was already in bed in the corner cubicle, watched them wistfully out of the corner of her eye. The term was more than half-way through and she still felt the odd one of the four. It wasn't as if she hadn't tried pretty hard to be more tidy and not so selfish. She could see clearly that she must have been pretty awful when she first came to Westways. No wonder Terry had detested her.

Only that morning Susan had received a letter from her mother and her vivid description of their latest water-hole party had carried her back to Rhodesia in spirit. How very far removed she felt from the girl who had lived there; from the time when, like all the other European children, she had dropped her things about just as she pleased, sure in the arrogant knowledge that the native servant would gladly tidy up after her. They ought not to let children be brought up like that. It made it dreadfully hard when they came to England.

'Lights out!' sang Lesley's pleasant voice from the doorway. 'Everyone ready? Good night.'

Though Susan's thoughts were just a trifle gloomy, they were not sufficiently so as to keep her awake for long; but in the next room, where Beryl had the cubicle by the window, it was a different story. Whisky's owner was feeling very miserable. Over and over again her mind went back to the events of the afternoon. But it was not the fright he had given her, but Whisky himself that worried her. She had told the other girls that she hated her pony, but when they got back to the stables after her disastrous experience and she had seen Masters shake his head gravely when Whisky still shivered, she had known that it was not true. She loved Whisky. Loved him terribly, and always would, even if he wasn't a champion jumper. Supposing anything should happen to him because of the afternoon's experience! She had heard of horses even dying of a chill. Supposing Whisky died! It would really be all her fault, because she knew that she ought to have been able to control him and stop him from running into the bog.

If only she had listened to Masters and learned to train her pony properly! The thought made Beryl more restless than ever and she tossed and turned uncomfortably in her bed until the light had faded and there was no sound but that of her room-mates breathing. At last she could endure it no longer. Slipping quietly out of bed she stood by the window looking out across the garden. The night was warm, the darkness of the sky lit with a sprinkling of stars, and the moon was rising.

Suddenly Beryl noticed another light. It flickered through the trees at the end of the garden and she knew at once that it came from the direction of the stables. Beryl's heart did a double somersault with fear. Perhaps Whisky was very ill—perhaps, even, dying! She couldn't bear it. He was her pony and she must know about him.

With sudden decision Beryl slid her feet into her shoes and cautiously removing her coat from the wardrobe slipped her arms into it and tiptoed from the room. On the landing it was very dark indeed and as she felt her way along the corridor and down the stairs with careful feet, a part of Beryl's mind speculated wildly on what would happen if one of the mistresses heard her, and what she would do if she could not unlock the door. The thought of Whisky's plight, however, dominated every difficulty and gave her courage to go on.

Creeping along the hall to the door leading into the garden, Beryl cautiously withdrew the bolts. Then holding her breath she turned the key, and opening the door, let herself out into the night. It was colder than she had expected, and Beryl drew her coat around her closer, then flitting like a dark shadow across the lawn and through the orchard, she paused uncertainly a few yards from the stables. Yes, the light came from there all right and she could hear voices. Pressing herself closely against the wall, she edged along it to the window where the light shone brightest.

Now she could see the top of Masters' grey head and Tom's brown one. Then she heard Masters say gravely:

'There, we've done all we can for him now, Tom. The little chap may recover, of course, but how it looks to me now is he may not last until the morning.'

Beryl drew in her breath sharply. Whisky mustn't, shouldn't, die without her seeing him! She couldn't bear it. Going round to the stable door, she slipped quickly into the nearest loose box, flattening herself against the wall as Jimmy moved restlessly. She put a soothing hand on his neck and he stood still. Beryl held her breath as she heard the two men move towards the door and Masters say:

'Douse the light now, lad. We must get some sleep.'

Then the door closed with a sharp click. Beryl started forward. Somehow it hadn't occurred to her that she would be locked in. She had a horrible moment of indecision, but she knew that if she revealed herself now Masters would send her straight back to bed. The desire to see Whisky overrode everything else, and she resigned herself to spending the rest of the night in the stable. Her eyes were getting more used to the darkness now, and through the window she could see the moon still rising. It gave her a sense of comfort.

Counting the loose boxes until she found the one in which her own pony was, Beryl opened the door and strained her eyes to peer through the dim light. She whispered softly:

'Whisky . . . Whisky, darling.'

Her hands groped through the air, and she could hear the sound of the pony's breathing, harsh and difficult. He was lying on a bed of straw and covered with a blanket. Beryl slipped down beside him and stroked him gently.

'Oh, Whisky darling, don't die, please! I'm sorry I've been so nasty to you. It's my fault—every bit of it. I'm not as good a rider as I thought I was, and I wouldn't take Masters' advice. I guess I've trained you all wrong and got you muddled up. But if only you'll get well I'll try and do better, and . . . and you can be the worst jumper in the world, if you like.'

Whisky gave a long shuddering sigh and lifted his head. In the moonlight Beryl could see the whites of his eyes as he rolled them pathetically towards her. She had the feeling, suddenly, that he liked to have her there.

Seating herself on the soft straw beside him, she took the pony's head on her knee and stroked it gently, speaking to him encouragingly in low tones. Was it her fancy that his breathing grew less laboured? Beryl settled herself more comfortably with her back against the wall. She tried not to think about what would happen in the morning when they found her there. If Whisky was glad for her to be there she didn't care, and if he got better because of it she would take any punishment they liked to give her.

She smoothed Whisky's head, and the rhythm of the movement was soothing. Presently her eyelids dropped gently and her head fell back against the wall. Both Beryl and her pony were fast asleep.

Hours later the grinding sound of the key in the lock disturbed Beryl a little, and a moment later Masters' startled ejaculation roused her fully. She opened her eyes. The morning sunlight was pouring through the window above her, and over the doorway of the loose box Masters' lined and ruddy face was staring at her with such a horrified expression that she almost laughed.

'Miss Beryl! Whatever are you doing here?'

Beryl stretched herself stiffly. Becoming conscious of the weight in her lap, she looked down with a sense of panic. Had Whisky died, then, in the night? But no, the pony slowly shook his head, then stumbled to his feet with a little whinny of welcome for the old groom.

'He's better?' Beryl implored the old man, as his gnarled hands ran gently over Whisky, feeling him all over.

For one awful moment Beryl thought he was going to say no, his expression was so grave.

'He's better. Much better . . . but . . .' Masters hesitated. 'I don't know how you got in here, Miss Beryl, but I do know that you're going to get into trouble. I'm afraid I'll have to tell Miss Duncan about this.'

Beryl threw up her head defiantly.

'If Whisky is better, then I don't care what happens. I came down here in the night just before you and Tom left. I thought Whisky was going to die, and I couldn't bear him to without me seeing him. But, oh, Masters, don't you think me being here might have made all the difference?' she finished appealingly.

Surely there was a little twinkle in Masters' eyes?

'Maybe. Hosses is knowing creatures; not so different from human beings, I guess, in wanting to matter a lot to someone.'

Beryl's eyes shone.

'Oh, Masters, Whisky does matter to me so much! I didn't know how much.' She hesitated. 'I'm sorry I've been so . . . so pig-headed. Please will you help me to train Whisky better when he's quite well?'

Masters held out a gnarled hand.

'Indeed I will, Miss Beryl. And I'd like to shake hands with you for being brave enough to admit that you've been . . . well, what you said.' Masters grinned. 'Now,' he went on half-apologetically, 'I'm afraid you'll have to come up with me to the school.'

Beryl turned for a last lingering look at the black pony, now standing patiently with his head over the door of his box.

'Good-bye, Whisky darling! He is going to be all right, isn't he, Masters?'

'Yes. Quite all right, I imagine.'

'Then I don't care what happens, as I said!' Beryl drew her coat around her and walked through the garden beside the old groom, her step jaunty and her chin tilted. As they reached the door of the school building she gave a great yawn.

'You can't imagine how tired and stiff I am. A stable may be all right for a pony, but not for me.'

Masters turned one of his quizzical looks on her and smiled wryly. Then he put out his hand and rang the bell sharply.

A sleepy-looking maid opened the door after a long interval and stared, her round eyes travelling swiftly downwards to the pyjama-clad legs appearing below Beryl's coat.

'Mercy me, why, Miss Beryl . . . !' she exclaimed.

'I know it's only half past six, Annie,' began Masters, 'but would Miss Duncan be awake, do you think? I ought to have a word with her.'

The maid gave Beryl another curious look.

'I'll just see. Miss Duncan usually wakes pretty early.'

Beryl sat on a chair just inside the door waiting meekly. She did not feel very worried. Miss Duncan loved horses. Surely she would understand?

A few minutes later the Headmistress came down the stairs, wearing a flowered house-coat, her hair neatly arranged, her face fresh and lightly powdered. Beryl had a great admiration for her at that moment. It seemed that nothing could shatter Miss Duncan's calm, for even when she heard that one of her pupils had spent the night in the stables with a sick horse she showed little surprise and certainly no horror.

'Thank you for coming, Masters. I'm glad to hear that Whisky is so much better. That is one very good thing.' Her grey eyes swept over Beryl with a considering expression. 'Well, Beryl?'

Beryl coloured hotly and twisted her hands together, feeling suddenly uncertain of herself.

'I . . . I suppose it was awfully wrong of me to do it,' she said, 'but, Miss Duncan, please, I *can't* say I'm sorry because . . . because Whisky is better and . . . and I sort of feel it was partly because I was there.'

'I see.' Miss Duncan's voice was gravely calm. 'Well, child, you look very tired and we cannot discuss anything now. Come, I'll get you a glass of milk and a biscuit and then you must go back to bed.'

Beryl drank the hot milk soberly and then followed Miss Duncan up to her dormitory. The other three occupants of the room, only just awake, watched the spectacle with round eyes. Whatever had Beryl been doing out of bed at that time of the morning with her coat on, and her shoes all wet too? But their curiosity was not to be satisfied then, at least.

'Beryl,' said Miss Duncan, drawing the cubicle curtains, 'you are not to speak a word to the others. And girls, leave Beryl alone and try to be as quiet as possible when you get up so that she can get some sleep. I put you on your honour.'

When the Headmistress had gone out of the room there was a long silence. Only Pat Hemmings permitted herself at least a slight expression of all their wondering conjectures.

'Well . . . !' she said, and left it at that.


## 14

## Gone!

'My dears!' Terry stood poised in the doorway of their room, her face alight with impish excitement. '*Have* you seen Fenella this morning?'

'No . . . why?' Jennifer and Elizabeth asked together, while Susan's face assumed the wary expression which often came over it when Fenella was discussed.

'She has some new glasses—nice ones with flesh-coloured rims! They make her look quite human.'

'Dear me!' Jennifer looked impressed. 'I must say she's coming on!'

'She certainly looks much nicer with that deep wave in the front of her hair,' put in Elizabeth. She giggled. 'We never thought to have our Sergeant-Major glamourized, did we?'

Terry looked thoughtful.

'I've just realized,' she said slowly, 'that there isn't so much of the sergeant-major about her these days. In fact,' she went on in a surprised voice, 'I believe I'm really beginning to quite like her!'

Susan did not dare to add her quota to the conversation after all the teasing she had endured because of her championship of Fenella, but she glowed with pleasure inwardly at Terry's remark. Fenella certainly was coming on!

But thoughts of Fenella were banished with dramatic suddenness, for now behind Terry in the doorway was Sheila Clark in her grooming-overall. Her face was flushed and her voice breathless as she exclaimed:

'I had to come and tell you, Terry! Firebrand has gone!'

'Gone? Gone where . . . ?' The four voices clamoured questions in varying tones of horror.

Sheila nodded gloomily and shrugged.

'Just gone—stolen, Masters believes. We didn't notice anything wrong when we first got down to the stables because, as you know, we usually leave Firebrand until the last, as Masters or Tom often sees to him. Then Ann opened the door with the key and the box was empty!'

Terry sat back on her bed with a stunned expression.

'But who could have stolen him? And why did they only take Firebrand?'

Sheila shook her head.

'Masters says there has been quite a lot of thieving around here. Of course, anyone who knew anything about horses would take Firebrand because he's really valuable, and, anyway, it would be difficult to take a whole batch of horses at once.'

'It's a good thing they didn't take Whisky as well,' remarked Jennifer. 'I think Beryl would have had hysterics. She's absolutely dotty about him since his illness and you know she didn't mind her punishment a bit and said it was worth it.'

'Poor Miss Duncan!' Elizabeth said unsteadily. 'She'll be terribly upset. Does she know?'

'Masters is with her now. He said something about 'phoning the police.'

'The Gymkhana won't be the same without Firebrand. He always wins prizes in the showing-class,' Jennifer remarked gloomily.

Terry turned on her fiercely.

'Tiny! What does the Gymkhana matter compared with Miss Duncan's loss? Surely the police will do something? Didn't Masters or Tom hear anything in the night? You said the stable door was locked?'

'Yes, it was . . . at least, we're almost sure it was. You know how absent-minded Ann is, and she got flustered when Masters questioned her and said she was sure she had to turn the key, but if he asked her any more she would begin to wonder if she had made a mistake.'

'How idiotic!' Terry said contemptuously.

'Yes, wasn't it? But you know what Ann is. Anyway, Tom swears he locked up last night. Well, I'd better get on. The breakfast-bell will ring in a minute and I've still got to change.' Sheila wheeled about quickly and ran along to her own room.

As the girls came out of their rooms a few minutes later to go down to breakfast it was obvious that the bad news had spread quickly. Along the wide polished hall leading to the dining-room the buzz of talk swelled to a crescendo, so much that Fenella, marshalling them through the doorway, had to raise her voice to make herself heard.

'Quietly, quietly, *please,* girls!' she admonished.

Though her voice had authority, it held a more pleasant note than it had done at one time, and the girls seemed to accept her ruling with little resentment. For a moment the hubbub died down, but when grace had been said and the girls had taken their seats, it broke out again, though in a subdued form. On every side one heard the words 'Firebrand', 'police' and 'stolen', while Form Three, whose turn it had been for grooming that morning and who had made the discovery of the loss, were regarded somewhat enviously as likely to have more details than those who only received the news secondhand.

Susan sat silent and thoughtful throughout the

meal. While Sheila had been talking upstairs, a sudden idea had occurred to her and it would not be dismissed. Though she told herself many times that it was wild and improbable, she could not get out of her head the feeling that Tom, the stable-boy, was somehow mixed up in this. She remembered the older man who had been arguing with him, his nasty shifty eyes and furtive expression, and how Tom had denied knowing him at all. She remembered, too, the silly question about the sheep and Tom's uneasy look when she had reminded him of it.

Then there was that sudden bilious attack which had prevented Tom from accompanying them on their ride across the moor; the ride on which Beryl had come to grief. It was strange that when they returned Tom should have seemed perfectly fit again. Could he have stayed behind on purpose to meet that man again, to scheme and plan for this theft?

Against all this, Susan thought of Tom's devotion to all the horses. Stupid though he seemed sometimes, it was obvious that he loved them all. It would be cruel to throw suspicion on him without more reason. Perhaps she was just imaginative and silly. Susan determined to forget about Tom.

But she couldn't forget about Firebrand. In class that morning Susan was rebuked several times for inattention. Miss Carr went so far as to express the opinion that she was disappointed.

'You've been doing so well lately, Susan. Don't begin to slack again.'

In spite of the rebuke Susan couldn't help feeling

pleased that Miss Carr thought she had really improved. It was certainly true that the extra coaching and Fenella's help had made lessons seem easier and more interesting, and now the horrid possibility of being relegated to a lower Form had faded a little. Remembering this, Susan tried hard to give her mind to the lesson, but in spite of her efforts her thoughts kept slipping away to Firebrand's empty stable. She wondered what Miss Duncan was feeling like, and guessed that her loss must have been a bitter blow to her.

Susan looked across at Terry, and knew that she too was miserable and worried. Terry loved all the horses so much. She would be feeling Miss Duncan's loss more than most. Terry looked up and they exchanged a glance. It seemed to Susan that in that look she and Terry were closer than they had ever been, and the thought pleased her. Then she caught Miss Carr's eye upon her again and, flushing guiltily, made another determined effort to concentrate.

All through the day conjectures were made about what was happening. Miss Duncan remained invisible and there was no more news. Susan envied those whose names were down for riding that afternoon because they, at least, might learn something. She decided, after school was over, to go down to the stables in any case. She was supposed to play netball, but she hoped they would not miss her enough to search for her. At the back of her mind was the feeling that if only she could see Tom and speak to him, she would know; know whether he had anything to do with the disappearance of Firebrand or not.

But Susan's plan was doomed to failure. As she ran down the garden she saw Hazel, who pounced on her before she could escape and reproached her bitterly.

'I'm as keen on horses and riding as anyone,' Hazel scolded, 'but even a school like Westways can't afford to spend all its time on it. We're getting badly left behind in our matches with other schools this year, and if I can't get more co-operation from you younger ones I'm going to speak to Miss Duncan about it.'

'But, Hazel——' began Susan.

'But nothing,' Hazel said firmly, propelling Susan towards the netball-ground. 'In any case, all those who were down on the list today are already out in the field and Masters has had enough company this afternoon. What with the loss of Firebrand and the police inquiries, he's quite upset, poor old man.'

Susan looked sulky and Hazel threw her a shrewd look.

'I thought you'd got out of that, Susan,' she said teasingly, and Susan looked ashamed of herself and tried to smile. The older girl went on encouragingly: 'I'm going to try you as shooter again. We need one badly in your Form and you did quite well the other day.'

So Susan found herself playing netball. Terry, who was almost as enthusiastic about games as she was about horses, was playing centre forward. Susan took up her position near the goal, but at first the play was mostly down the other end and she was inclined to dream. Suddenly she heard Terry shout:

'Look out, Susan!'

The ball was coming her way. She put out her hands and caught it. Though she was now some distance from the goal she lifted her arm and, with no great hope of success, shot the ball upwards. No one was more surprised than she when, after a convulsive wriggle on the ring, it settled and slipped through the net.

'I say, that was jolly good!' Terry's voice sang out spontaneously and Susan flushed, pleased. She told herself that it had only been a fluke, but now her enthusiasm was rising and, putting all thoughts of Firebrand out of her mind, she threw herself into the game, seizing the ball at every opportunity and surprising herself as well as the others by making two other telling shots at the goal. When play came to an end she was almost sorry, and felt that all this time she had been missing something.

'Pretty good, Susan,' Hazel told her approvingly. 'You're going to make a very good shooter, I think.'

Susan felt pleased at the praise, but now that the game was over her thoughts returned to Firebrand. She could see the girls who had been riding going into the school. In a few minutes the bell would be ringing to summon them to tea and she would have to be very quick if she was to get down to the stables. She ran across the field and through the orchard. Then her feet halted uncertainly, for coming towards her was Miss Duncan herself: Miss Duncan and a man in a trilby hat and a raincoat. He looked like a detective. They halted in front of her, and Miss Duncan raised her eyebrows inquiringly. Susan thought she looked very pale and worried.

'Yes, Susan? Did you want me?'

'N—no, Miss Duncan. I was just going down to the stables—to—to . . . just to have a look at Cobber.'

Miss Duncan took hold of Susan's arm and gently turned her in the opposite direction.

'There is no time for that now,' she said firmly. 'It is almost tea-time, and I imagine'—her glance fell on Susan's grubby hands with a hint of amusement—'that your hands require some attention before the meal.'

'But——' began Susan, desperately racking her brains for a genuine excuse.

Miss Duncan's mouth took a firmer expression. 'Run along,' she said, in a voice which brooked no argument.

Susan gave in despairingly. How was she to talk to Tom if no one would let her go to the stables? she wondered disconsolately. As she went in to the school building she met Beryl, who was full of her prowess that afternoon, though there was a new humility in her manner.

'Whisky is quite fit again now,' she told Susan happily. 'Masters has been giving me a real lesson—I asked him to, you know. I can see now that I was training Whisky in quite the wrong way, but Masters says I'm getting on very quickly. I expect I frightened him by holding his mouth too tightly. I always used to think you had to hang on tight to the reins, but Masters says you ought to hold them as if they were silk! Today I tried it that way, and Whisky jumped the sacks in fine style. Susan, don't you think horses are almost human? I'm sure Whisky feels quite differently to me since that awful night.'

'I'm awfully glad about it,' Susan said sincerely. She liked Beryl at that moment better than she had ever done. She linked an arm in hers as they went upstairs.

'Was there any news about Firebrand?' she asked anxiously. 'I tried to get down to the stables, but first Hazel made me play netball and then I met Miss Duncan and she said it was too late.'

Beryl shook her head.

'I don't think they've discovered anything really helpful,' she said. 'Miss Duncan came down to the field with a man and they called Masters away from me and were talking to him for quite a long time. Afterwards I saw them with Tom. I suppose he was something to do with the police.'

'Yes, I saw him. I thought he looked rather like a detective. What did Masters say . . . and Tom? Could you hear?'

'No, I couldn't hear a thing; they didn't mean us to, I expect. Of course we tried to get something out of Masters, but he was cross and wouldn't say anything. I think he's dreadfully upset. He looks almost ill.'

'And didn't you ask Tom if he knew what the police suggested?'

'Oh, of course we tried to pump him, but I think he'd been told not to talk to us, and he just shook his head and looked miserable. I think he feels responsible because it was he who locked up, but I do know that Masters stuck up for him and said he distinctly remembers Tom giving him the key last night, and in any case it was still on his ring when Ann asked him for it. Ann is all of a flummox now because she says she doesn't think now that she had to turn the key to open the door, but the lock isn't broken or anything. I looked myself.'

'It's a mystery,' sighed Susan. 'I say, I must get along. I've got to wash my hands yet. Oh, heavens, there's the tea-bell!'

Susan fled along the corridor in a panic. There was always the chance that a late arrival at a meal might carry a penalty of a cancelled ride.

## 15

## Suspicion

IN spite of the gloom which hung over the school regarding the disappearance of Firebrand, schooling the horses for the Gymkhana went on with unabated enthusiasm. 'After all,' as Terry said quite truly, 'if we sat down and cried all day it wouldn't help to bring Firebrand back.'

All the same the girls hoped daily for news that the police inquiries were having some success. One could see, although she did her best to hide it, that Miss Duncan was terribly distressed by her loss; and as for Masters, he was 'like a bear with a sore head'.

Beryl bewailed his impatience with bitterness.

'I really thought he meant to help me,' she complained, 'but now he gets in a temper with me when I do something wrong, although I try awfully hard to do everything he tells me.'

'It's not you,' Susan consoled her. 'The poor old chap feels all this so badly. I expect he thinks Miss Duncan blames him, although I'm sure she wouldn't really. Look, Beryl, would you let me help you a bit?' Susan was fast learning a becoming modesty, and she hastened to add, lest Beryl should think she was conceited: 'You see, I've been riding ever since I could walk. It isn't any credit to me. It's just a matter of circumstances.'

'You and Terry,' said Beryl enviously, 'are the best riders in the school.'

Susan glanced across to the other side of the field where Terry was painstakingly jumping Dallas over the wall.

'That's the fourth time she's done it without a fault,' she remarked. She swallowed hard, then admitted generously, 'Terry's better than me, I think.'

'Or Dallas is better than Cobber,' suggested Beryl. 'You've done wonders with him, but he does make a lot of faults.'

'I know,' Susan said briefly, not wanting to enter into a discussion on the merits of the two ponies. Cobber was her 'special'. She accepted and loved him just as he was, though she still had the uncomfortable feeling that he had been a better jumper before his fall. She was sorry for his decline only because she blamed herself for it and was jealous for his reputation. 'Come on, Beryl,' she said, lightly changing the subject now. 'You take Whisky over the brush and I'll tell you if I think there's anything you could improve.'

Beryl jumped the brush twice in fine style and then went on to the double bar. Whisky refused twice, but she was gentle with him and he cleared it at the third try.

'He'll do finely with just a bit more practice,' Susan encouraged, as Beryl rode towards her flushed with triumph. 'I'm awfully glad Whisky is improving because I always thought he was a fine little chap. I do think Masters was right and he hadn't been very well trained.'

Beryl leaned over to pat the glossy black neck, pleased by Susan's praise.

'Thanks, Susan. I think I'll just take him round the field for a canter and then I'll try him with the "in and out".'

Susan watched her go, then glanced round the field at the other ponies. Apart from Terry on Dallas, there was no one she could really count as a rival. Jennifer was fairly proficient on Nigger, but he was an untidy jumper and erratic. The trouble with most of the school ponies was that they were on the small side. Elizabeth was, as usual, on the stout Meggie, who was entirely undistinguished, but for her mildness and good temper. She had the kindest of eyes, two white feet and a long mane and tail. Susan watched her now with some amusement. Meggie carried her burden with patience rather than grace. When it came to the jumps she made an effort and just scraped over if she felt like it; but if she didn't, no amount of prodding would move her. She just stood quite still and turned her head over her shoulder with a benign expression. As Elizabeth often said, 'How *could* you scold her?'

Dumpling's too big for her, Susan decided now, just as Fenella was too big for Jimmy really, only somehow one laughs at Dumpling all the time in quite a different way from anyone else.

'I'm simply terrified of the bigger horses!' Elizabeth would say with mock alarm when the others suggested a change. 'I tell you what I want is a really nice cart-horse, big and docile. I'd get my father to buy me one, only he's as poor as a church mouse, the darling, like most clergymen.'

She never seemed to mind a bit, but then, Elizabeth never seemed to mind anything. She was always cheerful and good-tempered. It's nice to be like that, reflected Susan, and was ashamed to think how often she felt cross and snappy, though she thought she had been a little better lately. Then she shook herself mentally. This won't win Cobber rosettes at the Gymkhana! she admonished herself. Mounting her pony, she took him triumphantly over the brush and the double bar. He knocked down the triple and displaced two bricks from the wall.

'Not bad,' she told him, and fought down her sense of disappointment. Her mind went back to the day when Cobber had taken the gate in the field, with inches to spare. Would he ever jump like that again? Susan gave up putting him through his paces and practised mounting and dismounting. After all, the speed and neatness with which she accomplished this was very important in a Gymkhana. She had set her heart on jumping Cobber, but for all she knew now she might have him only for Musical Chairs or something like that.

From the direction of the stables a whistle blew; it was Masters' intimation that time was up. Susan rode Cobber across the field and, dismounting in the cobbled yard, led him to his box. She took off his saddle and bridle and gave him a good rub down.

'There you are, old chap, I must go in now,' she told him. 'Masters will bring you your supper presently. See you soon!' She put an arm round the pony's neck with an affectionate little squeeze, then sauntered out. The other ponies were being settled in and she was the first to finish.

Susan stood leaning against the wall remembering how strange she had felt on that first evening at Westways when she had come down to the stables with Elizabeth. It seemed a very long time ago, and it gave her a faint sense of shame to realize that if she were now to receive a summons from her mother and father to join them in Rhodesia it would not give her the delight it once would have done. In fact it would be almost a blow. She would love to see her parents, of course, but Westways was dear to her and she was part of it.

She wandered over to Firebrand's empty stable and wondered, as they all so often did, where he was and what had happened to him.

The other girls had not noticed Susan standing there waiting, and now she saw them all going up the garden together, Terry, with Elizabeth and Jennifer one on each side of her, Beryl arm-in-arm with Pat, the others straggling behind. Susan started after them, and at that moment Tom rounded the corner, his arms circling a bundle of hay. Susan had not seen him much since Firebrand's disappearance, and the suspicion which had been in her mind that day had almost faded. Now, as Tom's blue eyes met hers swiftly and as swiftly looked away, it flared again. She had the strangest feeling that Tom was frightened; that he thought she knew something about him. On an impulse she moved quickly over to him and, her her eyes holding his, said quickly :

'What about that man I saw you with in the field? Have you seen him again?'

It was a shot in the dark, but the result confirmed Susan's suspicion that Tom was hiding something. A dark red flush appeared above the collar of Tom's open-necked shirt and spread slowly upwards, and though he blustered he could not meet Susan's eyes.

'What's the idea, miss? You asked me about that

once before. I tell you I don't know the man. I never saw him before.' Then his manner altered and he laughed shortly. 'Been reading detective stories, miss? What crime are you trying to pin on me, eh?'

Susan hesitated. She really had nothing much to go on. She felt a little ridiculous as she walked away with what dignity she could muster. All the same, she thought, as she went slowly towards the school, she was going to keep a strict eye on Tom and see if she could find out anything about him that was suspicious. She felt almost sure that he had something to do with Firebrand's disappearance, but unless she had some more definite proof she couldn't tell anyone about it. They would laugh at her.

It was Susan's evening for studying with Fenella. She sat in front of her books, unable to concentrate. She looked up and, staring at Fenella's bent head, found herself thinking of that first evening. It was no good saying that appearance didn't make any difference, reflected Susan, noticing again how the new glasses seemed to lighten Fenella's face and how the soft wave now covered the too-high forehead. These improvements, added to a slightly softer manner and a more tolerant attitude, had made most of the girls decide that Fenella, after all, wasn't at all a bad sort. Susan hoped it would be her turn to visit Jacqueline again soon, so that she could tell her about it. She would be wiser, perhaps, not to put such a thing into a letter.

Fenella turned suddenly, aware of the Junior's scrutiny, and her face flushed.

'A penny for them, Susan,' she said lightly.

It was Susan's turn to blush.

'You'd think it was cheek . . .' she murmured.

Curiosity overcame Fenella's scruples and she probed:

'I guess it wasn't about your homework?'

'No,' confessed Susan simply. 'It was about you.' There was a little pause, then Susan went on awkwardly, 'I was thinking how nice you looked.'

Fenella flushed again, but Susan could see that she was pleased, though she wouldn't say so, of course. She cleared her throat and said gruffly:

'Well, what about your arithmetic? Let's have a look at what you've done so far.'

Silently Susan held out the book. Fenella raised her eyebrows at the sparsely filled page.

'Better get a move on,' she advised, and turned to her work again. For half an hour there was silence while Susan made up for lost time. Even when Fenella, at the end of that time, went through Susan's homework there was still a little constraint between them, but she smiled when she passed back the book.

'Congratulations, Susan. Every one right today. You're coming along so fast that you soon won't need my help.'

Susan gathered her books together and stood up. She backed towards the door with something of her old awkwardness.

'Good night, Fenella. Thank you.'

She raised her eyes. Fenella's grey ones had a twinkle in them. She smiled.

'Good night, Susan, and—and thank *you*.'

Susan fled. Outside the door her thoughts switched quickly away from Fenella again and back to her suspicions of Tom. How was she to find out anything else about him? She went slowly downstairs and put her books into her desk.

'Who's coming to see my stamps?' called Terry. 'I've got some new swops. Jolly good ones.'

The others crowded round her, and Susan managed to slip away into the garden unseen. It wasn't that she didn't want their company, and she would have liked to have seen the stamps; but now it was her duty to watch Tom, and the only way to do that was to go down to the stables and keep her eyes and ears open.

Sometimes during the brief period between prep and bedtime Susan would massage Cobber's legs with a circular movement of her hand because Masters had said that might strengthen them. For the lack of any more active ideas and the hope that she might see or hear something, Susan went in to Cobber and, squatting beside him on a wooden box, she massaged the leg which had once gone lame. Everything seemed very quiet, and she remembered hearing someone say that Masters was not at all well and the doctor had said he must stay in bed for a couple of days. She supposed Tom must have gone off somewhere, too.

Well, anyway, she wasn't actually wasting her time, because Cobber always seemed to like her massaging his leg and she was ready to do anything that might help him. The little sense of disappointment from his poor showing at the jumps that afternoon was still with her, and she could not get out of her head the realization that if Cobber had been able to do so much better before his fall, then she was to blame. As she moved her hand rhythmically across his fetlocks and up to his knee, Susan told herself that she would give almost anything to live again that day when she had jumped the gate so rashly. For it was then that she had lamed Cobber and taken the heart out of his jumping, and then, also, that she had upset Terry and made herself disliked.

Had she lived that down? Sometimes she thought she had, and then something would happen which would make her feel an outsider again. In a wild flight of fancy she saw herself making Cobber the finest jumper in England and then delivering him over to Terry so that she could win all the prizes. That sort of thing didn't, however, happen in real life. Susan sighed and stood up, giving a last-minute caress to Cobber's shining chestnut neck.

'Good night, old boy. I must go now.'

Susan suddenly realized that she had been sitting there dreaming for some time and that several minutes ago the school bell and the clatter of feet had announced supper-time. She must hurry. She turned to leave the stables and, as she did so, she heard someone coming in her direction. On an impulse Susan darted into Cobber's box again and flattened herself against the wall. The footsteps halted and there was a long, low whistle. Cautiously Susan peered out of the dusty window beside Cobber's head, then drew back swiftly. In that one brief moment she had recognized the thick tweed suit, the black hair and shifty eyes of the man she had seen talking to Tom. So Tom did know him after all!

The whistle came again, more prolonged this time, and then Susan heard Tom's peculiar limping step and a low murmur of voices. She edged herself carefully along the wall towards them. Whatever happened she must hear what they were saying!

## 16

## Suspicions Confirmed

IT was maddening not to be able to hear. She must! Susan threw caution to the winds and edged along the wall, almost to the doorway. Then Cobber moved restlessly behind her and she stepped back for a moment to quiet him.

'Please, darling, keep still,' she prayed him silently in her mind. 'It's so awfully important.'

Back near the door again Susan strained her ears towards the murmured conversation, and now she could distinctly hear Tom's voice, frightened and resentful.

'. . . You shouldn't have come here . . .'

Then the other man's voice, louder and gruffer:

'I promised you a split, didn't I?'

'Yes, I know you did, but I don't want it.'

'Nonsense, what are you playing at? I tell you no one would recognize the horse now. He took the colour beautifully and, though it's been the dickens of a job to fix it up, he's being shipped early tomorrow morning.' The man's voice grew angrier. 'You're a fine nephew, you are! What's the idea, anyway? I thought as how the fuss would have died down here by now. Have they been asking you questions? What did you tell 'em?'

'Questions . . . ! They've asked all the questions they can and I ain't said nothing. I wish I hadn't listened to you, that's all, uncle or no uncle. I don't want your filthy money.' Tom's voice was as miserable as it could be. The man's now took on a jaunty tone.

'Go on with you, lad. When there's been a bit of an interval we'll have another go. One or two nice little "thoroughs" you got here.'

'No, never any more. Get out o' here before I loses my temper and tells on yer.'

Susan was almost choking with excitement, her heart beating with such loud thumps that it seemed as if the two men outside must hear. Tom had evidently abandoned the argument and was leaving his companion. She could hear his feet limping away while the other man cursed softly. Susan's weight was distributed unevenly on her two feet, and suddenly her left leg was seized with dreadful pins-and-needles. She moved a foot restlessly and caught it against a bucket. It fell over with a crash. For a moment Susan thought she would faint with suspense and fright. Then suddenly the man pounced round the corner of the door and saw her.

'So it's young nosy-parker again? You little wretch!' The words hissed through his half-closed mouth with a venom that frightened Susan. She stared at him wild-eyed for a moment. Then she began to run.

The man caught her before she had gone more than a few yards and picking her up, struggling, carried her back into the stable. It had not somehow occurred to Susan to scream but, as she faced the man, panting, he seized her handkerchief, which was protruding from her pocket, and rammed it into her mouth. Again she tried to dart away. Again she was caught. Picking up a piece of rope from the corner of the stable, the man tied her feet and hands. He rammed the handkerchief farther into her mouth, just as she almost succeeded in dislodging it with her tongue, and tied it in with another rope so tightly that it hurt the back of her neck.

Susan's eyes glared at him fiercely. Though she was badly frightened she was conscious only of fury. How dared this hateful horrid man steal Firebrand, because of course it was obvious that he had. And how dared he tie her up like this! He needn't think he was going to get away with it. Not if she knew it. The man looked down at Susan furiously as she twisted and turned desperately, managing to catch him a sharp dig in the side with her elbow.

'Keep still, you little spitfire!' he muttered.

His small eyes roamed round the stable questioningly. Then he appeared to make a decision. Picking Susan up again and carrying her under his arm like a package, he moved towards the door. Glancing this way and that cautiously, he darted across the yard and through the gate into the field where the girls schooled the ponies. In the far corner was a small wooden shed which had once housed a pet goat. It was empty now, damp and rather smelly. Into this Susan was thrust roughly. She shuddered a little as the man deposited her on the straw in the corner, but her eyes still glared defiantly. The man stood looking down at her with a grim expression.

'There you are, young lady. The night is warm and someone will find you, no doubt, eventually. Let's hope they just give me time to get the horse and myself across the water. Cheerio! Sleep well.' He grinned evilly, showing discoloured teeth. Susan gave a desperate wriggle. She heard his footsteps dying away into the distance and felt an utter hopelessness sweep over her.

To cheer herself up, Susan told herself that soon her absence would be discovered, but another thought followed miserably. Who would ever think of looking for her in such a place? No one would come into the field until tomorrow afternoon, at the earliest, and by that time all hope of saving Firebrand would be gone. Poor Firebrand, he had been dyed another colour and tomorrow morning would have left the country. There would be small chance then of getting him back. Poor Miss Duncan, too! Susan sighed heavily. If only she could think of something to do!

She moved restlessly, the smell of the rotting straw so near her nose an added trial. She twirled her tied feet round and banged them against the wooden walls of the hut, but the small sound they made, she realized hopelessly, would not be heard more than a few yards away. She twisted herself again experimentally, and found that by heaving her legs and seat alternately she could move a few inches at a time. She persevered at this for some time, but progress was slow and painful. Realizing that it would take her hours and hours to cross the field, get through the gate and up to the school, she gave up the idea as hopeless and tried to think of another way. Something moved in the straw a few feet away from her and she shivered. It wasn't that she was afraid of field-mice and spiders, but presently it would be dark and it wouldn't be very nice if one ran across her face in the night! She began to hum snatches of song to keep up her courage, for the thought of the night had gripped her nerves. She mustn't panic. She must think of something else.

Susan's eyes roamed hopelessly round the small shed. She had manœuvred herself opposite the doorway now and from her lowly position she could see across the field. She looked longingly at the tall chimneys of Westways rising high above the trees. The upper windows of the house were just visible. Surely they must be looking for her? If only someone would go up to the attics with a pair of field-glasses they might be able to see her. She could imagine them saying, 'What is that dark bundle in the doorway of the hut in the field?' Susan laughed a little at the impossibility of the idea. They would look for her down at the stables, of course, and in the school, but why should they dream of her being in the shed where the goat had been?

Susan's eyes roamed around once more. She had almost sunk into despair when she saw the scythe.

It was leaning against the fence some ten yards away. Susan had heard Masters grumbling at Tom for leaving the tools about, but now she blessed his carelessness. With renewed hope she began her painful progress towards the scythe. It seemed hours before she lay, panting, beside it. It had a sharp curved blade and a long wooden handle. It would cut her ropes all right, if only she could bring the two together. At first it seemed hopeless, though Susan twisted herself like a contortionist in every direction. Then she had a brainwave. She kicked out with her tied legs until the scythe fell flat on the ground. Then almost lying on it she dragged herself so that the rope around her ankles met the blade. To and fro, up and down, went her legs. She could not get much pressure, and at intervals she had to pause, breathless and exhausted, but looking downwards anxiously she could see that the rope now showed distinct signs of fraying. How long it took Susan did not know, but when she was almost exhausted, there was a slackening of the tension and suddenly her legs were free! They felt very stiff and as if they did not belong to her, but by moving them up and down and round and round the circulation gradually came back until at last she was standing, if shakily, on her feet.

So busy had she been releasing herself that Susan had as yet made no plan. Now she reflected that if she went back the stable way Tom might see her, guess what had happened, and stop her. She couldn't believe that Tom would want to hurt her, but he was in this business, after all, and she couldn't afford to waste any more time.

Side-tracking the gate for safety, Susan slipped through a gap in the hedge which brought her into a corner of the orchard. She thought she must look a sorry sight with the handkerchief in her mouth, her hands tied behind her back and straw in her clothes and her hair. Stumbling often in her haste, she sped across the garden and in through the back door, almost colliding with Fenella, who was hurrying along the hall, an anxious expression on her face.

'Susan . . . !' Fenella almost screeched the name, then, recovering her usual brusque calm, wasted no more words. She swiftly untied the knot which kept the handkerchief in Susan's mouth and then released her arms. 'Don't talk for a moment,' she ordered. 'Come up to my room.'

Clinging to Fenella's arm, Susan obeyed and sank thankfully into a chair in the corner of Fenella's study. In truth she couldn't possibly have said a word. Her mouth felt dry and parched and her lips stiff and cracked. She moved her jaws painfully up and down and rubbed them gently with her sore hands. Fenella had run out of the room, and now she returned with a glass of water.

'Sip it slowly,' she directed. 'I've told Miss Duncan you're here.' She steadied the glass with her own hand when Susan's wobbled. The cool water tasted wonderful.

A few minutes later Miss Duncan hurried into the room.

'My dear child!' she exclaimed. 'We've all been so worried about you!'

Susan began to talk excitedly, and then the most absurd thing happened. The story she wanted to tell would not come out for sobs, and the tears began to pour down her face. She could do nothing but gasp and cry. For a few minutes she lost all control of herself. She was vaguely conscious of Miss Duncan holding her hand and saying soothing words and then Matron was beside her, holding a glass to her lips. She gulped down something with a bitter taste and felt better. Becoming quieter she realized, with something of a shock, that she was leaning against Fenella and that the older girl was smoothing her hair and saying soft, comforting things in a way Susan wouldn't have dreamed possible.

'Now, Susan,' said Miss Duncan quietly, 'if you could just manage to tell us what has happened, you'll be able to get to bed and rest.'

Susan made a big effort.

'It's Firebrand, Miss Duncan. The man who stole

him caught me listening. He tied me up and—and put me in the goat-shed. I cut the rope around my legs with a scythe which was in the field, but it took ages. . . .' Tears threatened to engulf Susan again. Fenella took her hand gently.

'Who was this man, Susan? Do you know?'

'He's T—Tom's uncle. And . . . and . . . he's had Firebrand dyed and he's being shipped abroad to-morrow morning. Oh, you must do something to save him, Miss Duncan!'

'We will. Don't worry, dear.' Miss Duncan soothed her. She loked puzzled and incredulous. 'You say *Tom* helped to do this?' her voice hardened.

Susan gulped.

'Yes, he did. But—but please don't be too hard on him, Miss Duncan. His uncle is a horrible man and he must have persuaded him into it. And Tom wouldn't take the money. You will remember that, won't you? Oh, Miss Duncan, *do* you think you'll be able to get Firebrand back?'

'We'll have a good try.' Miss Duncan looked very stern, her lips in a straight line. 'And he's been dyed, you say. My poor Firebrand . . . his beautiful coat . . . ! Fenella, get the police station on the tele-phone in my study, please. I'll be there in a moment. Would you like to sleep in the sick-room tonight, Susan? Everyone else is in bed, of course.'

'Oh, please . . . couldn't I sleep in my own room?' Susan's eyes were pleading, and after throwing an inquiring look at Matron and receiving a little nod, Miss Duncan gave in.

'All right, child, as you wish. Maybe you'll have a better night that way. Now good night. Matron, you'll warn the others not to talk too long?' Miss Duncan hurried from the room, and Matron took Susan along to her dormitory. She was still feeling very stiff and a little shaky, but she just couldn't help enjoying the sensation when Matron put on the light and three heads shot up from their pillows and three pairs of eyes stared at her excitedly. As Susan went to her own cubicle, Matron said quietly:

'Now, girls, Susan has had a very uncomfortable experience. Perhaps you will help her to bed while I go and get her a light supper. She must be needing it. I expect she will want to tell you all about it. Don't let her talk too much or get too excited. I'm sure you'll be sensible and thoughtful and insist that she doesn't.'

It was certainly a strange experience for Susan to be helped to bed by the other three girls. Between bites of her sandwiches and sips of milk she told them the whole story, and they hung on her words. After the fright and anxiety of her capture, it was comforting to be fussed over and treated like a heroine, quite apart from her intense hope that she would be instrumental in getting Firebrand back for Miss Duncan.

'We just couldn't think what could have happened to you!' Terry hung Susan's blazer on its hanger and dashed to forestall Jennifer's taking her empty mug. 'We've been lying awake for ages, thinking of everything.'

'And of course Terry had you practically dead and buried. You know what her imagination is,' Elizabeth said, her dimples deepening.

'Wasn't it you who had her as a stowaway on a boat to Rhodesia?' asked Terry indignantly. 'Anyway, Susan, we're jolly glad you're here now. Gosh, it must have been pretty awful in that vile, smelly little hut!'

'How did that man steal Firebrand?' wondered Jennifer. 'Do you think Tom unlocked the door for him?'

'I don't know exactly.' Susan looked thoughtful. 'Perhaps he really did lock up and then got the key off Masters' ring during the night. Ann certainly got the key from Masters all right. Anyway, I can't help hoping they let him off lightly. He wouldn't take the money his uncle offered him, and he sounded ever so fed-up about it. He's the most horrible man . . .' Susan shuddered. 'You ought to have seen him.'

'Look . . .' said Terry suddenly, 'don't you think we ought to leave Susan alone now? She's been an awful brick, but she must be dead tired, and we don't want her to look like a ghost tomorrow after all she's been through. I vote we don't any of us talk any more.'

'All right, Grandma!' Elizabeth grinned, and jumping into bed, pulled the bedclothes up round her neck. 'I feel a little like I do on Christmas Eve. You know, one wants to get to sleep as quickly as possible to make the morning come quicker. It's all so exciting!'

Terry paused before getting into bed herself.

'I say, Susan . . . if you wake up in the night . . . you know . . . feel scared or anything, you'll wake us, won't you?'

The question gave Susan a warm little feeling of pleasure. To have Terry asking her like that!

'M'm. I will,' she agreed. 'But really, I don't feel a bit sleepy. I guess I'll find it hard to go off tonight.'

A few minutes later Terry, thinking of some point she wanted cleared up, broke her own rule and asked Susan a question. Receiving no reply she raised herself on her elbow and listened to Susan's quiet, even breathing. They giggled, and Terry sighed philosophically.

'She's off already! I guess Matron must have given her something. Oh, well, my question can wait. Good night, you others!'

## 17

## A New Foursome

SUSAN awoke next morning to find the other three creeping about the room, trying to make as little noise as possible. She started up, alarmed.

'Oh, is it very late? Why didn't you call me?'

'Matron came in and told us to let you sleep as long as possible,' Terry informed her, adding teasingly, 'you are now enjoying the privileges of the famous.'

'What nonsense! I'm perfectly all right, and I want to hear about Firebrand as soon as possible.' Susan jumped out of bed quickly. 'Ouch! I am a bit stiff everywhere. . . .'

'Do you think you ought . . . ?' began Elizabeth. but Susan only grinned at her and told her not to be stuffy. She was ready almost as soon as the others and they formed a bodyguard around her as they went down to breakfast, feeling rather pleased with themselves that probably they alone knew the details of the events of the previous evening.

The main points of the affair were obviously common knowledge, however, and there was no getting away from the fact that Susan was the heroine of the occasion. If once she had felt herself unpopular, now she could have no doubts but that it was true no longer. In fact it was a trifle embarrassing, the attention she received. When breakfast was over, the girls crowded round begging her again and again for details.

'I don't know how you dared!' breathed little Carol Murray of the Second Form.

Susan laughed.

'I didn't dare anything,' she declared. 'It just happened to me and I couldn't get out of it.'

Fenella came hurrying through the door. Her eyebrows lifted whe she saw the crowd around Susan and her most authoritative manner came to the fore as she dispersed it.

'Have you girls nothing to do but bother Susan? What about your rooms this morning?'

The girls scuttled in various directions with no delay. Though they might like Fenella more these days, they still had a healthy dread of her wrath. Susan started off with the rest, but Fenella's hand on her shoulder detained her.

'Miss Duncan would like to see you, Susan,' she said more gently.

Susan's eyes widened.

'Oh, Fenella, have they found Firebrand?'

'Not yet. But come along, Miss Duncan will tell you about it.'

With inward impatience Susan suffered Miss Duncan's inquiries about how she had slept and how she was feeling.

'I'm really quite all right, Miss Duncan, thank you, except for just a slight stiffness. But . . . Firebrand?' Susan's eyes implored for news.

Miss Duncan looked down at the letters on her desk. Susan thought there had been tears in her eyes, but her voice was quite steady when she lifted her head again.

'I have no news yet. I am hoping to hear something quite soon.'

Susan bit her lip, looking worried.

'And Tom . . . what did he say about it?'

Miss Duncan shook her head. Her voice was rather sad.

'Tom . . . has run away. Apparently he couldn't face the music. The police found a note in his room.

It was addressed to me and was somewhat incoherent. He begged me to forgive him and told me how much he loved all the horses. It would have meant nothing to us had you not found out the rest of the story.'

'But . . . but where can he have gone?'

Miss Duncan's voice hardened.

'To join his uncle probably and share in the profits of his shady dealing.'

'Oh no . . . Tom wouldn't do that. . . .' Susan looked earnest. 'I'm sure he hates that horrid man. He sounded ever so miserable and sorry. . . .'

'Well, dear, I hope you are right. If the police catch up with this man and Tom is with him I am afraid it will go badly with him. However, we shall see.'

It seemed that Miss Duncan had finished with Susan, but she was loath to go. If only the telephone would ring while she was there so that she would know at once if Firebrand had been found! As she hesitated, searching for some question which would prolong the interview, there came a sharp knock on the door and a moment later it was thrown open. In the doorway stood Tom, dishevelled, dirty and untidy. He looked very tired and there were bits of grass and leaves on his clothes as though he had slept out all night.

'Tom!' Miss Duncan exclaimed, and Susan gasped.

Scarcely seeming to notice Susan, Tom limped forward. His blue eyes, red-rimmed and tired-looking, gazed anxiously at Miss Duncan.

'I had to come back, Miss Duncan . . . . You know

what I done?' His mouth quivered, then hardened. 'Uncle asked me, and I told him over and over I couldn't do it. . . . Guess I've always been kind of frightened of him. . . .' A sob broke Tom's voice. He plunged on desperately. 'I . . . I let him get Firebrand, and I ain't had a moment's peace since. I thought it'd be better if I got out, but that weren't no good . . . so I've come back, Miss Duncan, and you can do what you likes with me. I'd get Firebrand back for you if I knew how, but I don't. . . .'

'Sit down, Tom.' Miss Duncan's voice was kind.

Tom raised his head wearily. He passed a hand across his eyes as he sank into a chair.

'Ay, I guess I'm tired. I been walking about most of the night. . . .'

Miss Duncan bent forward.

'The police are looking for your uncle now,' she said slowly. 'Are you willing to help them by answering their questions?'

Tom's eyes grew eager.

'I'll help 'em all I know. . . .' Then his face fell. 'But there's nothing I can do to help,' he went on desperately. 'I wouldn't ask Uncle where he was taking Firebrand. I couldn't. I only knows he's shipping him across the water this morning.'

'Nevertheless, I think we ought to let them know.' Miss Duncan's hand went towards the telephone, then she looked across at Susan as if she had suddenly remembered her. 'Susan, I want you to ask Matron to make some substantial sandwiches and a hot drink. I'd like her to bring them down to Tom here, please.'

Susan's feet moved reluctantly to the door again. She threw a look of appeal over her shoulder, and hesitated.

'. . . I can come back, Miss Duncan?'

Miss Duncan's eyes held a look of amusement.

'I scarcely think we shall need you for this, dear. No, I think you had better join your class. Don't worry, Susan. You shall have the news as soon as possible,' she finished encouragingly.

Susan had no choice but to obey. She went downstairs and, after apologizing to the mistress in charge, took her seat at her desk in the Fourth Form classroom. Inquiring eyes followed her, and Susan shook her head to indicate that there was no news, but at break the others crowded round her, eager to hear what Miss Duncan had said, and intrigued by her story of Tom's sudden appearance.

'Do you think they will do anything to him?' asked Terry anxiously. 'After all, he confessed. I mean, he didn't know that Susan had found out about his uncle.'

Susan looked worried.

'I hope they don't punish him. He looked so really sorry. . . .'

All through the day excitement among the girls ran high, and the latest bulletins were passed from one to another. Someone had seen two policemen in the hall. Someone else had seen Tom get into a big car with another policeman. Masters had gone with him. And so on. . . . The mistresses were hard put to it to get any concentration from their pupils, and

Miss Martin, who took biology, and was elderly and prim, was heard openly to declare that Westways might be improved if *all* the horses were stolen, and for *good*. No one was seriously disturbed by this pronouncement. They were used to 'Marty's' rather acid remarks.

'Westways without the ponies! Why, it wouldn't *be* Westways!' declared Terry, voicing the feelings of everyone.

It was almost bedtime when Susan was sent for once more to Miss Duncan's study. She entered the room a little nervously. Was Miss Duncan going to tell her that the police had been unsuccessful? The moment she looked at the Headmistress's face, however, she knew that everything was all right.

'Ah, come in, Susan,' she said, smiling cheerfully. 'Yes, it's good news this time!'

'Oh, Miss Duncan . . . Firebrand . . . have they found Firebrand?' Susan asked breathlessly.

'Yes, my dear. There was some difficulty in finding out where he had been taken, for Tom quite genuinely knew nothing about his uncle's plans, or what part of the country Firebrand was to be shipped from. I'm afraid it would have been too late had not there been some delay in getting him away and the police, having at last discovered a clue, were able to arrest the thief early this afternoon.'

'And . . . and Firebrand is all right?'

Miss Duncan smiled wryly.

'All right in health, yes. I've just had a telephone message from Masters, who insisted on getting up and going down to identify Firebrand. It seems that he is now a muddy black colour—my beautiful cream-coloured horse! Isn't it a shame?'

'Oh, but won't they be able to get it off?' Susan clasped her hands earnestly.

'It is too early to say. It seems that an expert must decide if it is that kind of dye. You may be sure Masters will make every effort. You know what a pride he takes in Firebrand's appearance. Well, we mustn't think too much about that part of it, must we, Susan? In any case, his coat will grow again, and I'm lucky to get him back. And I have you to thank, Susan. I haven't said thank you yet, but I'd like to now.' Miss Duncan held out her hand her eyes were a little moist, though she still smiled.

Susan took the hand shyly.

'Honestly, I didn't do anything really, Miss Duncan. As I told the girls, it just happened to me. But all the same, I'm . . . I'm awfully glad.' Susan's bright face clouded suddenly, and Miss Duncan asked:

'What is it, Susan?'

'I'm . . . I was thinking about Tom. What will happen to him, Miss Duncan?'

Miss Duncan looked grave.

'Well, really, I don't quite know, but I've asked them not to be too hard on him. He was influenced by his uncle quite against his will. I'm sure of that.'

'Oh, I am too, Miss Duncan,' Susan agreed fervently. 'I heard them talking, you see, and I know Tom didn't like doing it. Will you . . . ?' She hesitated again, and Miss Duncan prompted:

'Will I . . . what, Susan?'

'Will you take him back here?' Susan's eyes were anxious.

'Yes. I've told him that I will. Masters has been pleading for him, too, and I mean to give him another chance.'

'Oh, *good*! I'm so glad. Then everything is all right, isn't it?' Susan's face showed her relief as she thankfully made her escape. She was longing to tell the others the good news and, nice as Miss Duncan was, she had seen enough of the Headmistress's study for one day.

Upstairs in Dormitory Ten the other three were already getting ready for bed. As Susan came along the corridor she could hear them giggling. They broke off as she entered the room, and Terry asked anxiously:

'Is there any news?'

Susan fought down the old feeling that they had been laughing about her. Everyone had been so nice to her lately. She mustn't be silly and sensitive.

'Yes,' she told them. 'The thief has been caught and Masters has identified Firebrand and is bringing him back.'

'Identified?' Terry snapped at the word anxiously. 'Isn't he all right?'

'Oh yes. Except that he's a horrid dark colour. Isn't it a shame? They dyed him so that no one would know . . . Miss Duncan says Masters may be able to get it off, though.'

Terry put an arm round Susan's waist and twirled her round the room until she was quite breathless.

'Stop it, Terry, for goodness' sake!'

'I'm so relieved, I must let off steam somehow!' Terry stopped suddenly and began to giggle again. The others joined in. 'Susan, we've thought of the funniest thing!'

Now they were all off again, stuffing their handkerchiefs in their mouths and rolling about on their beds in fits of laughter. Susan regarded them in bewilderment.

'Whatever *is* the matter?'

'We . . . we . . .' began Terry weakly, and just then the door opened quickly and Fenella stood there looking at them.

'Honestly,' she reproached them, 'I know things are a bit out of the rut at the moment, but really you must make less noise, girls.'

Terry wiped her eyes and made a great effort.

'I'm sorry, Fenella. We—we thought of something aw—awfully funny, but we really will try. . . .' She hiccupped, and the corners of Fenella's mouth curled upwards for a brief moment.

'You'd better try very hard. I'm warning you,' she said, and disappeared.

'You know,' said Jennifer wonderingly. 'I'm getting quite *fond* of Fenella!'

'She's changed,' said Terry.

'For the better,' agreed Elizabeth.

Susan didn't say anything, but her eyes shone. 'I

knew she'd do it . . . good old Fenella,' she thought, then aloud asked curiously:

'Do tell me what you were laughing at. That is, if you can without going off again,' she warned them.

Terry suppressed further giggles with a stupendous effort.

'We were talking about the time when Rosemary was here and we four called ourselves the Friendleebarlows. We were wondering if we couldn't think of another name to include you instead of Rosemary when——' She broke off, overcome again.

'When we suddenly realized that we would be——' Jennifer stuffed her handkerchief into her mouth and bit on it fiercely.

Elizabeth took a deep breath.

'Don't you see, Susan? We're now the Friendleebar*lambs*! Isn't it rich?'

In a few minutes they were helpless, all four of them, rolling about on the beds and burying their heads in their pillows to suppress the sound of their mirth. Through Susan's laughter one glorious thought was predominant. Now she had been accepted as one of them and was no longer the 'odd man out'. Her allegiance to the newly formed Friendleebarlambs should be fervent and undying.

If Fenella heard the further sounds of mirth from their dormitory, she was kind enough to ignore it for once. At last they began to feel better and Terry sat up and wiped her eyes resolutely.

'I feel like that song. You know. . . . The one that

begins, "I never cried so much in all me life!"' she said weakly.

'Don't . . . !' begged Elizabeth faintly. 'Let's talk about something else!'

'I can't think of anything but the Friendleebarlambs!' wailed Jennifer with a sniff.

'I can,' said Terry firmly. 'I'm going to think about the Gymkhana. That's serious enough, in all conscience! Listen girls, we've three more weeks in which to practise, and if the Friendleebarlambs (with perhaps a little help from one or two other Fourth-Formers) can't manage to walk off with the Form cup, then my name is not Terry Barton! What do you say?'

'But what can *I* do?' wailed Elizabeth. 'I'm the only one of you who is no good.'

Terry didn't attempt to deny it.

'If Fenella can improve, so can you, Dumpling,' she said severely. 'And in any case, we could perhaps concentrate on you for the Fancy Dress ride at the end.'

'Is there one? What fun!' Susan's eyes sparkled. 'I've just thought of what Dumpling could be—that is, if she doesn't mind,' she finished apologetically.

Elizabeth sighed.

'It's another insult, I'll be bound. However'—she lifted her eyes to the ceiling in mock resignation—'for the good of the cause I'll be anything, or do anything.'

'Hush!' warned Terry. 'I hear the patter of Prefect feet. Jump in, girls!'

175

All four girls jumped into their beds as though they were worked by clockwork, and drawing the bedclothes neatly up to their chins, lay meekly prone.

'Very pretty!' said Fenella's voice from the doorway. 'Good night, girls!'

'Good night, Fenella.' Four voices answered with deceptive gentleness. There was a long silence while the sound of Fenella's feet gradually died away. Then Terry sat up in bed.

'Susan, don't talk too loudly, but . . . do tell us . . .'

## 18

## The Gymkhana

THE day of the Gymkhana dawned fine and sunny. After the gloomy week of weather which had preceded the longed-for event, it seemed almost too good to be true and excitement swept to an even higher level.

'If only it lasts!' breathed Terry anxiously, standing by the dormitory window in her pyjamas and scanning the cloudless sky.

The Friendleebarlambs had sprung out of bed even before the first early call, for 'Fourths upwards' had been detailed for the important task of grooming the ponies for this special occasion. They hurried through their dressing with all speed and were first down at the stables.

'I'm *determined* to do Dallas myself,' declared Terry, hurrying towards his box. She turned and winked at the others. 'And of course, Susan will groom Meggie.'

Elizabeth giggled.

'No other hands but mine shall touch the little fat darling!' she said dramatically. 'But Susan may watch.'

Susan made a face at them and, laughing, went in to Cobber. She didn't mind their teasing now. In fact, looking back, she realized that she must have taken offence many times when none was intended.

Very soon the four girls were joined by other enthusiasts and the stables became a hive of activity. Never did saddles and bridles shine more darkly rich or bits and pieces sparkle more brightly. Manes and tails were plaited with special care in festive style, and each pony inspected carefully by an extremely critical and anxious Masters. The old groom seemed to be everywhere at once that morning, scolding, encouraging, advising. This was *his* day, and now that Miss Duncan's beloved Firebrand was back amongst them he was prepared to enjoy it to the full.

In the background hovered Tom. He had been put on probation by the Judge, who had sentenced his uncle for the theft of Firebrand, and looked so humble and anxious to please these days that everyone felt quite sorry for him. Susan took special trouble to ask his opinion of Cobber's appearance, and was rewarded by a grateful look and an enthusiastic rubbing of a saddle already polished to perfection.

By ten o'clock the whole school was assembled in the prepared field, and the girls, attired in jodhs and clean blue blouses, watched anxiously for the arrival of friends and relations. Susan was expecting Aunt Jane, and although that was nice, she suddenly felt a little bleak, remembering that she would be the only one of the Friendleebarlambs whose parents would not be there. She had been hoping this morning that a letter from hers would ease the little feeling of loneliness amongst all these other girls who were expecting mothers or fathers or both; but posts from South Africa seemed a little slack lately, and she had not had a letter for two weeks. She stood watching the busy scene for a moment, wishing for the impossible.

In the corner of the field was the Secretary's tent, and Susan could see several people arriving there to be welcomed by Miss Duncan and some of the other mistresses. In the collecting-ring now were many riders she did not know, for Westways' Horse Show and Gymkhana was an annual event and the proceeds were given to the local hospital, so that both those interested in watching and in riding had an encouragement or an excuse for putting in an appearance. Near the gate leading into the orchard a large marquee had been erected for refreshments, and Terry had informed Susan that even the girls were to have a buffet-lunch there. It was Susan's first introduction to an English show and, the weather having come up to scratch, she decided that, but for her own personal reservations, everything was quite perfect.

Now Terry was pulling at her arm.

'Come and meet Daddy,' she begged, and led her up to a large man with a jolly face. He shook Susan's hand with a clasp which left her limp. 'Mummy's coming along a bit later,' Terry explained. 'She gets bored with the showing-classes and likes the afternoon best.'

Susan suddenly caught sight of Aunt Jane and, excusing herself, rushed over to greet her and find her a good seat. Close by, a lady and gentleman were standing with their backs towards her, and as Susan kissed Aunt Jane something familiar about them clutched at her heart. But, of course, it couldn't be! Mummy and Daddy were in Rhodesia.

Almost breathless, she detached herself from Aunt Jane, tip-toed round them, and then flung herself upon them,

'Mummy . . . ! Daddy! Darlings . . . ! But how . . . why . . . what has happened to bring you here?'

Important as the Gymkhana was to Susan, common sense told her that couldn't be the only reason for their presence.

'We're in England, darling, for good.' Mrs. Lambert watched Susan's face through a mist of happy tears. 'Oh, Susan, that was why we got Aunt Jane to start you at Westways this term. There was this possibility ahead of us, and it seemed stupid to take you with us for so short a time. If it had been quite certain we would have told you, but we couldn't bear you to be looking forward to it and then to be disappointed.'

Susan's eyes were wide and shining.

'And it's really certain now?' She mustn't let herself go until she was absolutely sure. Aunt Jane was very nice, of course, but at the back of her mind she had felt very disconsolate at the thought of spending all the holidays alone with her while Mummy and Daddy were so far away. Her father nodded reassuringly.

'Yes. It's quite certain now. When you break up we shall all have a holiday together first. Then we must find a house to live in. I'd like to get somewhere fairly near here because my work now is centred at Exeter.'

'But, Daddy, that's quite perfect!' Released from the vision of a stuffy suburban town like the one where Aunt Jane lived, Susan's prospects became even rosier. She gave a little skip of joy and hanging on to her father's arm squeezed it delightedly.

The sudden blast of a hunting-horn made them all jump and brought them back to their immediate surroundings. An old man in shabby hunting-clothes was standing just inside the ring, making the most of his opportunity. Mrs. Lambert put her hands over her ears and Susan laughed.

'That's the beginning. I'll have to leave you now for a bit. Will these seats do? Good-bye, darlings, for the moment!' Susan squeezed their hands again and ran on towards the collecting-ring, consulting her programme as she went. The first showing classes were for lightweight and heavyweight hunters, but after that would come the ponies and she had, miraculously, drawn the honour of riding Cobber. Of course he wouldn't win, the darling, but they should see that he could behave himself nicely.

'Look at Firebrand,' said Terry, spying Susan and dashing over towards her excitedly. 'You'd never know, would you?'

'He looks as beautiful as ever,' agreed Susan. 'Good old Masters!'

Terry stood beside Susan, giving her information. 'That's Lord Cambarthy—the fat man with a red face—he's one of the judges. He always comes. The other judge is the tall thin man with the nose—his name is Colonel Markham.'

The hunters were now being slowly ridden round the ring. Masters was riding Firebrand. The old man sat erect and proud. Susan guessed that Miss Duncan felt he deserved the honour, and so he did. Everyone knew how hard he had worked over Firebrand in the last two weeks. The dye had been analysed and treated, and now Firebrand's coat shone glossily cream as ever. He seemed almost conscious of his own beauty, and held his head at a proud angle.

Some of the other competitors were no mean rivals, Susan noticed, feeling a little anxious. There was a fine grey ridden by a haughty female in a well-cut habit, and a lady riding side-saddle with perfect poise on a spirited chestnut. A lanky youth with a very long neck looked stiff, but the brown horse he rode was well mannered and had some good points.

'Only four that matter,' muttered Terry shrewdly, dismissing the other entries with contempt.

Susan almost held her breath as the horses filed round the ring in procession, now trotting, now cantering. She felt she just couldn't bear it for Masters if Firebrand didn't win. The four that Terry and Susan had picked out were called into the ring. The judges rode solemnly round on each of them in turn; saddles were taken off, they were led in and out, fetlocks and quarters considered. Susan's hands were a trifle damp and she and Terry squeezed closer together for comfort.

'That grey will get it,' muttered Terry fiercely, willing it otherwise.

'She mustn't. Firebrand. Firebrand,' Susan hissed through her teeth.

The rosettes were in the judges' hands now. Lord Cambarthy hesitated only a minute longer. At a word from his colleague he went over to Masters and held up the coveted red rosette. Masters inclined his head in a dignified manner and, taking the rosette between his teeth, sat up very straight and correct.

'He's got it! He's got it!' Susan and Terry clasped each other in wild excitement, then, remembering their manners, tried to behave more decorously. They scarcely noticed that the blue rosette went to the grey, the yellow to the side-saddle chestnut and the white to the lanky boy's horse. As the four rode twice round the ring headed by Firebrand, the girls of Westways cheered and clapped and cheered again. It was not only because it was a triumph for the school. It was because they loved Miss Duncan and the old man who sat her horse now so correctly. Masters' face was serious and not particularly elated, as became an old hand at the game, but as he rode nearer to them, Susan saw a look in his eyes which satisfied her. Out of the corner of her eye she could see Tom, too, clapping wildly. Then his arm went up and he drew it quickly across his eyes. Susan looked away hastily.

The next two classes were for outsiders, and the girls of Westways gave them the polite attention one should give to visitors. Then came the pony class, open to all under sixteen. Susan was in the collecting-ring on Cobber, with Terry on Dallas. They looked at each other and smiled. 'Good luck!' they said together, well knowing they both would need more than that to beat some of the better-bred ponies belonging both to the school and to outsiders.

Cobber behaved well, and Dallas too. They were both shown off to their best advantage and admired by some, but from the first it was apparent that they were hopelessly outclassed. There was a girl there with a white pony which had everything on points, and she was called out almost at once. The judges were walking round, and one of the stewards beckoned to Beryl. Her face coloured hotly with excitement, but she kept her mouth straight as she rode Whisky forward. There were six ponies called out, three from the school and three outsiders.

'Good old Beryl! She's second,' said Terry. 'That's two points towards the Fourth Form getting the Cup, anyway.'

'Beryl's much nicer these days,' remarked Jennifer from behind them. 'At one time I'd have hated her to win anything because she had such a swelled head. Look, Sheila's reserve. I thought Lady Jane would have beaten that other black pony.'

By twelve o'clock all the showing classes were finished.

'The afternoon is even more exciting!' Susan said as she sat at a table in the marquee with her parents and her aunt. She munched sandwiches in contented anticipation, beaming at her mother and father and fussing a little over Aunt Jane so that she shouldn't feel neglected after all her kindness. Then she jumped up to introduce Terry, whose father had now been joined by Mrs. Barton, a pretty woman with Terry's smile. They made room for the others and sat chatting together.

'Did you get your wish, Susan?' Mr. Lambert's eyes twinkled across at his daughter knowingly. She nodded, smiling, and explained to the rest:

'Daddy knew how much I wanted to jump Cobber.'

'I think we'd both have *died* if we couldn't have jumped Cobber and Dallas!' Terry said dramatically.

'Dear me!' said Mr. Lambert, so seriously that Susan choked on her lemonade.

'Listen! They're going to begin again!' Terry

suddenly exclaimed, almost knocking over her chair with excitement. 'Come on, Susan!'

Everyone took their places to watch the open class for jumping, and Susan and Terry ran round to the collecting-ring side of the field in readiness for their own class. Miss Duncan was now up on Firebrand. The grey who had been second in the showing-class was good, it was obvious at once. Both she and Firebrand did a clear round the first time. There were several who made only one or two faults, but the rest of the class was mediocre. One weary black with a very cross rider stopped dead to nibble the furze, missed the gate and utterly abolished the wall, to ride off in disorder.

'Serve the man right,' said Terry crossly. 'He's horrid to that poor horse.'

While the rails and bricks were being replaced, she and Susan discussed Firebrand's chances.

'The grey is good,' Susan admitted rather sadly. 'I've a horrid feeling . . .'

'Firebrand won a first last year, but that grey wasn't here,' Terry said, obviously wishing the poor creature anywhere but at Westways.

As they feared, the grey came in first, with Firebrand second.

'Still a second is jolly good,' Terry said stoutly, clapping hard as Miss Duncan rode by, the blue rosette in her mouth.

Another small triumph came for the Fourth Form when Pat scored a first on Pegtop in the Potato Race.

'That's three more points. I thought Pegtop would

win that because she's so neat-footed,' said Terry, with the satisfied air of one whose predictions always come true.

'But you didn't dream Fenella would win a second in the bending, now did you?' teased Susan laughingly.

'No, I admit that. Of course, Muffet has always been pretty good, but I can't think how Fenella's managed to come on so quickly. I still have to laugh when I think of her on Jimmy at the beginning of the term.'

Someone standing just behind Susan nudged her gently. She turned quickly, and gasped a little.

'Oh, Jacqueline! I didn't know you were here!' Susan suddenly looked a little shy, remembering Terry's remark. Jacqueline drew her a little away from the others, and Susan asked quickly: 'Are you . . . are you all right now, Jacqueline? I should have asked at once.'

Jacqueline nodded smilingly.

'Yes, thank you, Susan. But I didn't come to talk about myself. I just wanted to thank you, Susan, for doing a difficult job well.'

'But honestly, I didn't do anything . . .'

Jacqueline smiled and nodded, then moved away to speak to someone else. Susan gazed after her, feeling proud and pleased. Of course she hadn't really done anything, but it had been nice of Jacqueline. . . . She turned back to the ring, and was in time to see Jennifer, flushed and triumphant, secure the last seat in Musical Chairs.

'Three more points,' said Terry, so absorbed in point-hoarding that she had not noticed Susan's absence.

Jennifer ran towards them, scarcely listening to their congratulations.

'It's the under-sixteen jumping now. We're depending on you two,' she told them.

'If one of you doesn't get a first you'll be expelled from the Friendleebarlambs!' threatened Elizabeth.

They went together to the collecting-ring, and Terry and Susan mounted their ponies. This was one of the most important events of the afternoon. There were eight girls jumping for Westways, two from each of the lower Forms and the same number of outsiders. Susan and Terry shook hands solemnly.

'Good luck!' said Susan, and meant it.

Terry winked.

'May the best man win!'

The steward handed her a number.

'Oh, gosh! I'm first,' Terry made a grimace.

'Number One!'

Terry rode Dallas forward at the command, and Susan leaned forward over Cobber.

'Come along, old beauty, here's where you do your stuff; the best you've ever done,' she whispered into the silken ear below her. She was ashamed at once of the way her heart sank a little when Dallas jumped a clear round. She didn't mind. She didn't. Everything was all right now between she and Terry. She could afford to be generous. She wanted Terry to win in a way . . . only she was going to do her best to beat her, because otherwise it wouldn't be fair to Cobber.

A boy jumped next on an infuriated-looking pony. He cleared the brush with a good deal of kicking, but when forced to rise at the double bar he knocked it down with such force that he nearly took a header into the spectators.

'Four faults!' roared the steward.

Susan was next. Blissfully unconscious of the amusement of those near enough to overhear her habit of murmuring, 'Ups-a-daisy!' to her pony at each jump, she did a clear round and drew in beside Terry feeling pleased with herself. She was keeping her end up—and Cobber's! She and Terry beamed at each other.

Several other good jumpers did clear rounds, but they could not repeat the performance. After ten minutes more the competitors were reduced to two— Terry and Susan. After doing three clear rounds, they then each made two faults. A little sigh went up from the onlookers and everyone grew tense. There was no great division of support for either girl. Terry was popular, but Susan's persistent training of Cobber and her experience with the man who stole Firebrand had captured their imagination. And they were both members of the Fourth Form.

'Go it, Terry! Go it, Susan!' the girls shouted alternately.

Terry went round again. No faults. Everyone clapped wildly, and people leaned forward, anxious not to miss anything.

Susan closed her eyes for a moment and told herself severely to keep calm. Then she collected Cobber expertly and he jumped each obstacle neatly. She could feel that he was enjoying himself now.

The crowds cheered. The stewards signalled Terry and Susan to wait a moment. They raised the bar to a triple and laid another row of bricks along the wall. Terry rode forward. Dallas' hind legs just caught the triple bar. It swayed and fell behind her, but otherwise it was a clear round.

'Two faults!' roared the steward.

Susan took a deep breath. She dared not think. 'Ups-a-daisy!' she shouted, and heard the triple clatter behind her. She rose again at the wall. She was over.

'Two faults . . .' The murmur ran round the field like an echo. Susan was shaking now.

Terry looked quite calm, but was she? She rode forward again. Again the triple clattered behind her. The steward's voice was quieter this time, and a hush hung over the field.

Susan leaned down and patted Cobber's neck. She wouldn't hurry him.

'Remember the gate in the field?' she whispered. 'You did that. This isn't any higher.'

As Susan rode forward she knew suddenly that it was going to be all right. She was very calm.

'Ups-a-daisy!' she sang out gladly, as she faced the triple again. Cobber rose with a great bound. He was up . . . up and over! A burst of clapping rang out, and was hushed again lest it should make Susan nervous at the wall. But nothing could stop Cobber now. He rode over the wall easily, making another clear round. A storm of clapping burst out. Susan had won.

As she rode into the centre of the ring for her rosette, Susan had a moment of reaction. Should she have tried so hard to beat Terry? But it wasn't she who had jumped so well—it was Cobber. She had given back to him his love of jumping, and he deserved his triumph. Half fearfully Susan glanced across at Terry and saw that it was all right. She was smiling at her behind her blue rosette.

'Two fine little ponies,' said Lord Cambarthy, patting them both and shaking hands warmly with the two girls, his red face one broad smile.

People had almost forgotten the two who had gained the yellow and the white rosettes, but they were given a hand as they rode back into the ring looking a little sheepish. But as the four rode round the field it was for Susan and Terry they clapped and cheered.

'Trained in South Africa, you know, on my Basuto ponies,' Mr. Lambert said proudly to anyone who would listen.

'Westways is pretty good,' remarked Mr. Barton, beaming.

Aunt Jane raised a laugh by asking plaintively, 'But I suppose they do teach them other things as well?'

'Oh, Aunt Jane, of course!' Susan said reproachully when the remark was repeated to her. 'And I'm actually going to have a prize this term!'

'For general improvement and good behaviour?' teased her father.

'Well, for general improvement, anyway,' Susan said demurely. Then she looked more serious. 'No, honestly, Daddy, I didn't like to tell you so in my letters, but at one time it looked as if I would have to be put down into a lower Form. I had to work very hard, but I had extra coaching and Fenella's help, and I got better.'

'Fenella? Oh yes, that was the pleasant-looking girl who was working so hard at lunch-time; the one with the deep voice.'

Terry and Susan looked at each other and grinned.

'Our sergeant-major . . .' said Terry under her breath.

'Sh!' warned Susan. 'We said we'd stop calling her that!'

'What's going on now?' asked Mrs. Lambert, looking over towards the collecting-ring from where came shouts of laughter.

'It's the last item, the Fancy Dress Ride,' said Susan. 'Terry and I are not in this. We've been busy getting Dumpling up for it, though.'

Into the field now rode a motley procession. There were jesters and knights of old, fair ladies and nursery characters; but the funniest of all was the fairy. Elizabeth's plump body was attired in the shortest and fluffiest of white frilly skirts and her shoulders bulged over a tight satin bodice ornamented by a pair of small gauzy wings. At a rakish angle on her head was a little wreath surmounted by a silver star beneath which her plump face beamed rosily. In her hand she held a tiny wand. Poor fat Meggie carried her burden so patiently and wearily that the whole effect was mirth-provoking, and people just rocked with laughter. Even the judges were wiping their eyes as, with no hesitation at all, they presented Elizabeth with the red rosette.

Slipping off her pony with a little flourish, she made a cute little curtsey, then ran over to Susan's group, laughing.

'Dumpling, you were simply marvellous!' Jennifer thumped her back while Susan and Terry dragged her forward to introduce her.

'It was my one chance,' explained Elizabeth, beaming at them. 'All four of us helped to make the costume. At least I can say now that the Friendlee-barlambs have all had a hand in winning the Cup for the Fourth Form. Because we have, you know, easily. Come on, girls, we have to collect.'

The four friends linked arms and strode over to the Secretary's tent where the prizes were to be distributed. The older folk followed them, and Mrs. Lambert said happily:

'I certainly didn't think that Susan would settle down in England so quickly and easily. I was afraid she would find things a little difficult.'

It was Aunt Jane's turn to put in a word.

'Didn't I tell you,' she said triumphantly, 'that Westways was the right school for Susan?'